SILVANO CASALDI

ANZIO-NETTUNO BEACHHEAD
January 22nd – May 26th 1944

WORLD WAR II
75TH Anniversary
Commemorative Edition

ANZIO-NETTUNO BEACH HEAD

Codice ISBN: 9781791590680
Independently published

I edition: December 2018

ANZIO-NETTUNO BEACH HEAD

*Humanity must
put an end to war
or war will
put an end to humanity.*
(John F. Kennedy,
*message to the
United Nations*,
25th September 1961)

ANZIO-NETTUNO BEACH HEAD

AKNOWLEDGEMENTS

I wish to express my gratitude to all publishers, writers, newspaper offices, magazines, news and photographic agencies, as well as archivist who have made this work possible with the material they have freely put at our disposal and authorized us to reproduce. This book, considering the reconstruction of events and in the intention of comparing the various interpretations of episodes most often discussed, is based on what has been published over the years by Winston Churchill, Generals Alexander, Clark, Lucas, Truscott, Penney, Kesserling and Westphal, Major Fehrenbach, Captain Bowditch and the Anglo-American war correspondents.

A particular word of thanks goes to:
-Churchill Literary Foundation, Putney House, Hopkinton, New Hampshire.
-Dr. Piero Cecchini, Agenzia Letteraria Internazionale, Milan.
-Raleigh Trevelyan, London.
-Professor Augusto Rondoni, Ernesto Rosi, Amerigo Salvini, Sergio Baldazzi, Paolo Blasimme, Nettuno.
-Dr Connie Heditsian, USIS Library, us Embassy, Rome.

-Dr Dilys Soria, British Council, Rome.
-John Frost, Historical Newspaper Service, London.
-Jean Paul Pallud, «After the Battle», London.
-Dr Edith Stark, Press Office, Embassy of West Germany, Rome.
-Prof. Piergiuseppe Bozzetti and Dr Stefano Giachini, Embassy of Italy, Washington.
-Dr Franca Alvisi, I.C.C.D. Library of Aerial Photographs, Rome.
-Dr Franco Lepri, Head of the Archives Department «Il Messaggero», Rome.
-Dr Luciana Quagliato, Mr Pasquale Antonio Di Todaro and Mrs Vita Vitali, «Corriere della Sera», Milan and Rome.
-Dr Josè Pellegrini, «Domenica del Corriere», Milan.
-Dr Benedetta De Matteis, Dr Giavanna Cordari and Mr Antonio Trincali, National Library, Rome.
-Roberto Rozzi, Anzio, Pavia Lewis, Cleveland, Ohio.
-National Archives Washington.
-Museum of the Smithsonian Institute, Washington.
-Imperial War Museum, London.
-British Library, Newspaper Library, London.
-German Archives, Koblenz.

FOREWORD

At two o' clock on the night of January 22nd, 1944 the 6th Corps under the command of General Lucas landed at Nettuno and Anzio. Immediately hope was born: a hope named Rome.

Official history has amply documented the course of the battle in which, for more than four months, an army contingent conceived by Churchill as a «wild cat» stayed riveted along the slopes of the Alban Hills and, in the disappointment of the time, came to be compared to a «stranded whale».

Certainly those months of "impasse" were a great disappointment. The Italian philosopher Benedetto Croce wrote about it in his diary on February 5th, 1944: «Unfortunately all hope of an imminent entry into Rome is lost, and even on the battle front the allied landings are coming to a stalemate».

It was a delay that cost blood, mourning and ruins. It was a severe blow to the Roman resistance, and the massacre at Fosse Ardeatine tragically sealed the Nazis' reaction against innocent lives. Those days that Nettuno and Anzio lived through were a tragedy for Italy and for Europe, almost a prelude to what four months later were to be the landing in Normandy. And it was to be right there in

ANZIO-NETTUNO BEACH HEAD

Normandy that the lesson learned and applied at Anzio and Nettuno were to bear fruits.

Today, in a world born out of that struggle and those sacrifices, we remember the hundred thousand Italians, including those who fell at Nettuno and Anzio, who died in the Liberation war: those martyrs, with their sacrifice, redeemed Italy's honor and laid down the premise by which our nation fully participates in the assembly of international bodies. That is how we feel today about those faraway events when history is conceived always as living history, never ending; because history dies only when we think of the present in terms of the past rather than of the past in terms of the present.

Of this new Italy, founded on civil, tolerant and democratic value, those days at Anzio-Nettuno were in a certain sense a foretaste.

GIOVANNI SPADOLINI
Chaiman of the Senate Republic of Italy

FOREWORD

Many years have passed since the Allies landed on the beaches of Anzio and Nettuno. The beachhead lasted from January 22nd to May 26th, 1944, and I think that most of us who fought there felt we would never want to return. Yet there is a strange compulsion to revisit battle sites, no to revive memories but has a kind of healing. And of course there is the need to see the graves of comrades who lie in the cemeteries. We grow old, but they shall not grow old. In our minds, and in the minds of those strangers who look upon the neat carved stones, each with names and rank, the bones beneath are forever youthful. The war cemeteries, scattered now throughout the world, are – or should be – silent pleas for tolerance and forgiveness.

I have found myself returning to Anzio and Nettuno several times, and have many friends there. The old battlefields have changed greatly, and that is to the good. Now I can even remember some moments of beauty in those months of 1944. The twin towns have become happy thriving places - places to enjoy. The physical scars have gone. I suppose half of the inhabitants never knew the war.

The British sector was to the north-west, and therefore to the British the Beachhead is synonymous with Anzio. Indeed it was as the Anzio Beachhead that he whole operation came subsequently to be known, presumably in the first instance, because Anzio had an harbor. The American sector was to the south, and therefore to American veterans the Beachhead will always mean both Nettuno and Anzio.

Nettuno has been overshadowed in the history of the Italian campaign. It is timely and just that Silvano Casaldi should have put the record right. The people of Nettuno also suffered greatly, and this deserves recognition by the world. The story in this book has also been illuminated and made more valuable by accounts of individual ordeals and act of bravery, some of them outstanding.

Silvano Casaldi has studied the campaign deeply and has read widely. He has also been able, through interviews, to produce fresh material of considerable interest to historians. He has reached his own conclusions on the Allies' strategy, and on the character of the political and military leaders. Any opinions about the whys and wherefores of the Beachhead, and the way it was conducted, are bound to be controversial. Some readers will applaud, some will disagree. All will salute the

ANZIO-NETTUNO BEACH HEAD

author's deep perception, his industry and above all his devotion to the people of Nettuno.

RALEIGH TREVELYAN
English writer and historian

ANZIO-NETTUNO BEACH HEAD

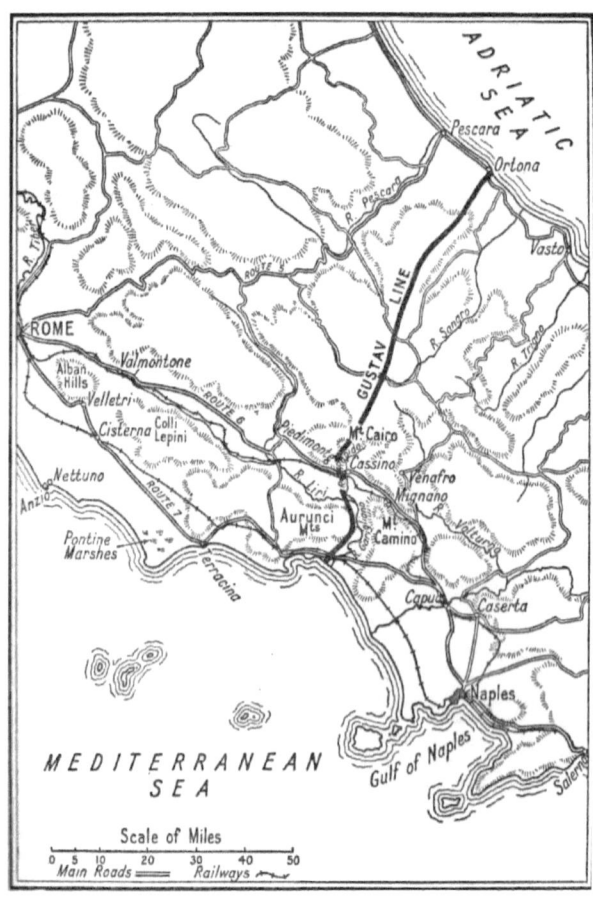

Stalemate in Italy, December 1943 – The Allies' slow advance up the Italian peninsula, where they had been forced to mark time by the Apennines barrier and the strongly fortified Gustav Line.

INTRODUCTION

The writing of this book has been an act of love towards Nettuno, which lived the greatest tragedy of its history with the wartime action, generally remembered as the Anzio Landing. Perhaps it is not exactly a book, in the sense that it seemed to me that I was writing the longest news coverage of my life. What spurred me was:

1) The fact that he name of Nettuno, so often quoted during the war, was afterwards ignored: so much so that, in November 1947, Mayor Mario De Franceschi had to intervene with the Ministry of the Interior before the people of Nettuno were able to share with the people of Anzio the aid that the city of Dunkirk, New York, had sent them. Hence, it is wrong to call the landing by the name of Anzio and it is also mistake to name it after Nettuno alone; it must be called either the Anzio-Nettuno Landing or else the Nettuno-Anzio one.
2) The iniquitous treatment meted out to General John Lucas. He was made responsible for those four months the Allies spent

at the beachhead; but the responsibility lay with others.
3) The bitterness of the survivors, so movingly expressed by the English historian Raleigh Trevelyan, in his book Rome '44. "At Anzio I had been a platoon commander, aged twenty, and like others around me had to believe that the discomforts and the deaths had a point, and that those in charge of our destinies knew what they were doing and never made mistakes, and that they were never affected by fatigue, vanity, jealousy or megalomania".
4) The capacity of free nations for criticism and self-criticism. "We Americans, wrote Major Theodore Reed Fehrenbach, do not recall the great victories but rather the hard times, the days that put our spirit to the test: Valley Forge, Alamo, Bastogne, Pork Chop Hill, Anzio".
5) Benedetto Croce's warning: "...As far as I am concerned I have reached the conclusion that this isn't a war for freedom, but, like all the others, it is for independence, for supremacy and economic and political advantage, and that the war for freedom will have to be fought later, and with more varied and appropriate means that arms".

6) Finally, the realization that history, called upon to give an account of a world war, cannot always dwell upon the affairs of a small community: our purpose is also to point out some of the more difficult situations each one has had to face vis-à-vis other cultures. The book has been translated into English in the hope that this will carry it beyond the confines of Nettuno. It is dedicated to all who died, particularly those who rest in the American cemetery at Nettuno, in the British cemeteries at Anzio and Falasche, in the German cemetery of Pomezia and in the Italian cemetery «Campo della Memoria» at Nettuno; it is offered as a gesture of fraternity.

Silvano Casaldi

ANZIO-NETTUNO BEACH HEAD

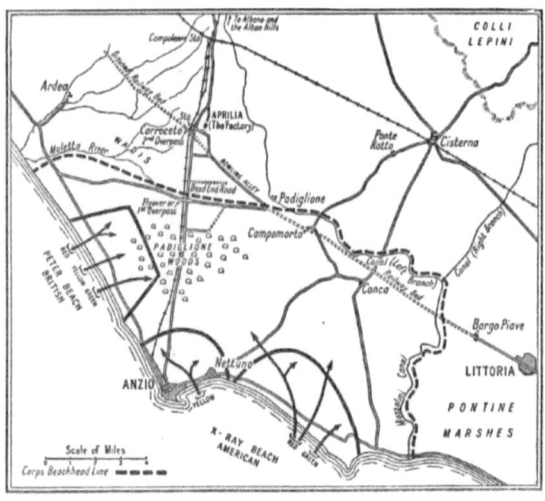

The landing, January 22nd, 1944 – Known as Task Force 81, the landing fleet included: 2 command ships, 4 Liberty, 8 LSI's, 84 LST's, 96 LCI's, 50 LCT's. As escort the English had 1 flagship, 4 cruisers, 14 destroyers, 2 anti-aircraft ships, 2 Dutch gunboats, 17 mine sweepers, 4 LC gun, 4 LC flak, 4 LC rockets. The Americans had 1 flagship, 1 cruiser, 10 destroyers, 6 mine sweepers, 32 submarine chasers, 6 repair ships. The American, X Ray beach, landed with three battalions from the 6615th Ranger Force, together with the 509th parachute battalion (yellow arrows) and the 7th, 15th, 30th Regiments of the 3rd Infantry Division (red and green arrows); the British, Peter beach, landed with the 2nd Brigade Group from the 1st Infantry Division (red arrow), the 24th Guards Brigades (yellow arrow), the 9th and 43rd Commandos (green arrow).

THE LANDING

At two o' clock, in the night of January 22nd, 1944, a Saturday, the 6th Corps, on the orders of US General John Porter Lucas, landed at Nettuno and Anzio. In those days these two towns on the Tyrrhenian coast, were named differently as in 1940 the Fascist regime had joined them together and imposed the single name of Nettunia. The 6th Corps, which was part of General Mark Wayne Clark's Fifth Army, comprised the US 3rd Division and the British 1st Division, both infantry and both reinforced with special units. Apart from occupying Nettuno with the 509th Parachute Battalion and the port of Anzio with three battalions of Rangers, the US 3rd Division under the command of General Lucien King Truscott, moved into the neighborhood of Foglino, Astura and the Mussolini Canal (the Moscarello today, near Foce Verde). The British 1st Division, under the command of General William Ronald Cambell Penney, came from the Eighth Army's Adriatic front and, augmented by the 9th and the 43rd Commandos, drew up along the coast west of Anzio, where the residential area of Lido dei Pini seaside resort have since grown up. It was the start of Operation Shingle, as the landing was code-named. (The word "shingle" refers to beach shingles, not roof tiles as has sometimes been suggested).

ANZIO-NETTUNO BEACH HEAD

FROM THE PONZA SIDE

Along the beach, from Nettuno-Anzio windows and terraces, especially on a summer evening, when dusk is falling and it would seems that the motionless sea, fading, is about to disappear, and then unexpectedly, on the already shadowy horizon the dark silhouette of a ferry-boat from Ponza, with its load of trippers, comes into view. And so, as often happens, as we wait to see it grow, draw nearer and take shape, our eyes fixed on it right until it berths at Anzio, we might well imagine that this was how the great fleet of Operation Shingle approached these shores.

And in fact that was just the route it took. The approach was made in the dark with the ships' lights blotted out. In preparing for the operation, minute care had already be taken in the bases of Naples and Salerno to disguise every movement. The Allies succeeded in keeping their operation hidden from the Germans, even though this was a matter of shipping an army of fifty thousand men, hundreds of amphibian and armored craft, tanks, artillery and thousands of trucks.

The fleet, which was divided into "X" Group (the American) and "P" Group (the British), also included Greek, French and Dutch naval units, a force of about 250 cargo and landing-crafts, five cruisers, about thirty destroyers and more and more than a hundred smaller boats. The ships set out not only from the two major ports of Salerno and Naples, but also from the small coastal towns in the Gulf; all of them were directed as if making for the south. (But there were four Liberty carrying heavier equipment which set out from Algeria.)

The American convoy had begun to ship anchor at dawn on January 21st. It was commanded by Admiral Frank J. Lowry, on board the "Biscayne"; he had been given charge of the whole operation. In the afternoon came the turn of the English convoy under Admiral Thomas H. Troubridge, on board the "Bulolo".

The sea was calm, and the forecast promised another three days of good weather. There was no sign of the enemy. Before evening, when it was feared that the movements and the converging of the fleet could no longer go unnoticed there was no sign of a single airplane of the Luftwaffe in the whole area. On deck, as they headed for the waters around Capri, everyone enjoyed the spectacle. The war correspondents, who were used to a situation which left no space for gushing, embellished their accounts with descriptions of the colors of the Sorrento coastline, and the smoke above Vesuvius as it faded into the distance.

The impression of a festive departure, which had been noticeable in Naples as the various divisions arrived for embarkation with their bands in the lead, was intensified as the fleet left the bay, while a very fast anti-torpedo boat wove in and among the ships with the signal flags fluttering. Standing upright on the M.T.B. was the Commander-in-Chief of the Allied Forces in Italy, General Alexander, who was saluting his soldiers and wishing them good fortune.

However, right up the last moment no effort was spared to deceive the observers on land, with whom the German spy service, were well-provided. Some of the lighter vessels followed a different route, sailing along the coast. It was with the same intention of side tracking the enemy that Terracina and Formia had been bombed on the 20th and 21st, and a cruiser and two anti-torpedo boats were sent to shell the port of Civitavecchia, shortly before zero hour in Anzio-Nettuno. The greater part of the fleet, however, after having simulated a voyage in the opposite direction, gathered together again over beyond Capri, and when the light of day had faded, suddenly switched course and headed north, making for Ischia and the Pontine Islands. From there it made for the mainland, just like the ferry-boat which return from Ponza every evening.

Without doubt it was Winston Churchill who took the closest interest in the landing. He was the Number One in the team which saved the world from Nazi-fascism. His fellow-countrymen, from the Queen downwards, have always acknowledged that he deserves a monument at least highest than Nelson's Column in Trafalgar Square, even despite the fact that in the elections of 1945, when his portrait was still hanging in almost every home as the national hero, the British electorate still had no hesitation in rejecting him in favor of Labor's Clement Attlee.

Given his strongly conservative leaning, Churchill must have been more adept at solving the problem of war than those of peace and social transformation. Even so he proved capable of turning the tables before disappearing from the political scene, and returning to Downing Street in 1951 as Prime Minister; proof of his resilient personality, which also found expression in other fields, including writing and painting.

In the case at hand, it was not so much his boxer's temperament as his intuition or even his ability as a statesman who knew how to unravel tangled knots, which proved his worth as a strategist. That in fact is what he was, with the tendency to gamble. Not for nothing had he been educated in a military academy where the use of ships was one of the first subjects taught. It is easy to understand his predilection for landings and more generally for all kinds of action based on audacity and unpredictable.

Not even the disastrous outcome of his Gallipoli landing in the First World War discouraged him. Accused of having imperiled the whole expedition to the Dardanelles, he was forced to resign as Secretary to the Admiralty in 1915, but without budging an inch from his convictions. With the cigar always jutting from his mouth, his invariable answer to difficulties, especially in the most dramatic situations, was to raise his two fingers in the V-sign. When he succeeded Chamberlain in May 1940, he became the symbol of contemptuous defiance to Hitler's threats and proposal, while France was surrendering, and England was rescuing the survivors of Dunkirk.

This greater gambler, impatient at the slow advance of the Allies up the Italian peninsula, where they had been forced to mark time by the Apennines barrier and the strongly fortified Gustav Line, could not fail to be gripped by the idea of a «wildcat strike», as he wrote, at the rear of the Germans. Eisenhower (the Supreme Allied Commander in the Mediterranean) and Alexander had already devised the scheme in November 1943 for the landing of a division south of the Tiber. This was supposed to be the knock-out punch when the Germans were with their backs to the ropes as a result of a massive attack along the whole 85 mile front from the Tyrrhenian to the Adriatic. For the landing which was always subject to the outcome of the main offensive, it was necessary to wait till Clark had opened the breach at Cassino, and arrived with the Fifth Army at Frosinone. This didn't happen, Nor were the Germans forced back to the ropes by the Eighth Army, where Montgomery also had the task of converging on Rome. So it was goodbye to Operation Shingle. In an official communiqué of 20th December, the plan was scrapped. This was also because Eisenhower had many other things on his mind; he was on the point of handing over his Mediterranean command to General Wilson, and moving to England to take charge of Operation Overlord, the Normandy Invasion.

We must picture Churchill who, on top of everything, was at this moment, far from well, despite the fact that he was in quite enchanting place: Eisenhower's villa. This seemed to have been chosen specially for the inspiration and rest of the old warrior, with its view of the Gulf of Tunis, the palms, the dazzling white of the houses bathed in sunlight, and, if that was not enough, the silence of the ruins of Carthage. But Churchill was bedridden with pneumonia, possibly caught during the Teheran conference (29th November – 1st December 1943) where he had discussed the latest moves in the war with Roosevelt and Stalin. If it had depended on the Kremlin dictator, the landing at Anzio and Nettuno would never have been taken place. He was demanding that the Allies should open the second front in France, and said the he would prefer to be on the defensive in Italy rather than think about taking Rome. Churchill writes: "I replied that we should be no stronger if we pulled out of the advance on Rome, and once we had taken the city we should be in a stronger position through having destroyed or badly mutilated ten or eleven German divisions. Moreover we required the airfield north of Rome for the bombing of Germany. It would be impossible for us to forgo the capture of Rome. To do so would be regarded on all sides as a crushing defeat, and the British Parliament would not tolerate the idea for the moment". (Churchill. *The second world war,* vol. 5, p. 314).

It was also a question of prestige, as we can see. But now that the December attack on the Italian front had come to nothing, how could he prevent Stalin's opinion from affecting his ally Roosevelt? His illness did not stop him from making his wishes known to the Chief of Staff with a service note which was a real telling off: "I am anxiously awaiting a full list of all landing-craft of all types in the Mediterranean now, showing their condition and employment, and especially whether it is true that a large number are absorbed in purely supply work to the prevention of their amphibious duties. These is no doubt that the stagnation of the whole campaign on the Italian front is becoming scandallous... The total neglect to provide amphibious action on the Adriatic side and the failure to strike any similar blow on the west have been disastrous". *(Churchill. Op.,cit.,* vol. 5 pp. 379-380*)*.

He took the matter up even more forcibly with Alexander, and this was only the first step in getting Operation Shingle back into action. After more than two millennia, the fate of Rome was again being decided on the shores of Carthage, though the positions were very different from those of Hannibal and Scipio Africanus.

 When he met the military chiefs at Christmas (the only absente were Clark and Lucas, the very men who were to have led the expedition), Churchill spared no effort to convince them. If at least two divisions were put ashore, the enemy forces would be put into difficulty and this in turn would help the Fifth Army to break through the Gustav Line, without having to wait until it advanced on its own as in the previous plan.

The gambler however was not one to be too tempted by the big stakes in poker to refrain from bluffing. Let us just say that in his manner of dealing with danger he had more of the bridge player in him; he never let go entirely of the safe game. Above all, in any case, the man's conscience was accustomed to answering for his actions. At the very moment that he got the go-ahead from Eisenhower, we find him expressing his scruples. According to him, it would necessary to use two British division, detached from the Eight Army in this operation: "I thought the amphibious operation involved potential mortal risk to the landed forces, and I preferred to run them with British troops, because it was to Britain that I was responsible". (Churchill, *Op. Cit.*, p. 385).

ANZIO-NETTUNO BEACH HEAD

From left: General Mark W. Clark, commander of the Fifth Army, General Lucian K. Truscott, commander of the 3rd Infantry Division and General John P. Lucas, commander of 6th Corps, make tribute to the Army by standing at attention while the band plays US Hymn. The last thing Clark said to Lucas in Naples before embarking was: "Don't stick your neck out, Johnny. I did at Salerno and got into trouble".

ANZIO-NETTUNO BEACH HEAD

Also General George S. Patton wanted to greet the troops before the invasion at Anzio-Nettuno. He was discouraged by what he learned that only two infantry division had the task to make the landings and blurted out: "John, there is no one in the Army I hate to see killed as much as you, but you can't get out of this alive".

ANZIO-NETTUNO BEACH HEAD

General Mark Clark on route to the beachhead, reads a message from General John Lucas. It is obvious from his air of serenity that there are no Germans around.

ANZIO-NETTUNO BEACH HEAD

General Harold R. L. G. Alexander, Allied Army Commander in Italy, at the harbor of Anzio on D-day. General Alexander seemed very enthusiastic of the operation and said to Lucas: "You have certainly given the folks at home something to talk about". In the background the white Casino of Anzio which was the headquarters of Colonel William Darby, the Rangers' commander.

ANZIO-NETTUNO BEACH HEAD

Soldiers of the American 3rd Infantry Division land in a hurry at Nettuno, on X-Ray Beach.

ANZIO-NETTUNO BEACH HEAD

In the calm of a perfect January morning the British land at Peter Beach, north of Anzio.

ANZIO-NETTUNO BEACH HEAD

Bob Kearney and Jack Malone from the 504th Parachute Infantry Regiment, wring out their clothes on the shore at Nettuno.

ANZIO-NETTUNO BEACH HEAD

A YES FROM THE WHITE HOUSE

Subsequently Alexander, having consulted with Clark and General Robertson, who was in charge of supplies, decided on one American and one British division. The problem remained of the amassing the landing-craft needed, they were already gathered in the Atlantic in preparation of the assault on the French coast. Churchill proposed, but it was Roosevelt who disposed. Would he be prepared to permit the indispensable landing-craft to remain a little longer in the Mediterranean, even at the risk of delaying the operation in the English channel? The vessels concerned were the huge floating carriers, capable of filling their bellies with extremely heavy tanks and whole battalions of infantry, and discharging them swiftly ashore with their forward hatched lowered.

Churchill was by no means confident. He admits that he was surprised and even overjoyed when he read the replay from the US President. It was a telegram, dated 28th December 1943. The first words left no possibility of doubt: "It is agreed to delay the departure of fifty-six L.S.I.'s scheduled for Overlord for mounting Anzio on January 20th...". (Churchill, *Op. Cit.*, p. 390).

In order to enter into Churchill's mind, we should also quote a passage from his Memoirs in which he defines what he calls the Moral of the Work: "In war: resolution; in defeat: defiance; in victory: magnanimity; in peace: goodwill". However, these sentiments did not preclude a touch of self-satisfaction in the strategist who, it should not be forgotten, had himself been trained for naval warfare in the Military Academy at Sandhurst.

He lost no time in expressing his satisfaction to Roosevelt: «I thank God for this fine decision, which engages us once again in wholehearted unity upon a great enterprise». He was sure of success, and when the go-ahead was given for the ship to embark, he probably gave way to the typical hasty gesture of the football fan who shout "Goal!" at the moment of the shot. On 21st January, that is, before the Rangers had reached the Zanardelli Riviera, or were in Via Gramsci, he had already wired to Stalin: "We have launched the big attack against the German armies defending Rome which I told you about at Teheran. The weather conditions seem favourable. I hope to have good news for you before long". (Churchill, *Op.Cit.*, p. 425).

Churchill was not wrong. Up to now he had played a sure hand, and he could be even more pleased with the fact that he had misled the enemy completely. That night before the naval rocket started to fire, all the Germans slept like babies in arms. "It did not seem possible", reported the BBC correspondent, "that the enemy was still unaware that a vest armada of ships: cruisers, destroyers, troop-carriers, minesweepers, landing-craft of all shapes and sizes, was now lying silent only two miles out of sea". (Vaughan-Thomas, *Anzio*, p. 2). This same correspondent, the Welsh broadcaster Wynford Vaughan-Thomas, the author of the book which has the highest readership among the people of Anzio and Nettuno, also received the order to disembark. He was calm. Before him, several waves of assault battalions had landed. In front of Anzio-Nettuno, The Rangers and paratroops in particular had been subjected to great tension by the wait on board the landing-craft, in which the thirty minutes before zero-hour or two o'clock, had been spent. The starlit night, with the sea caressed by a slight breeze, must have been one of those which suggest an expedition to fish for bream, or watch from the Belvedere the collection of the boats rocking gently to and fro in the open sea as they cast their lines into the deep.

The rocking of the landing-craft, however, was more of a shudder caused by the men's tension. Their anxiety was increased by the memory of Salerno where the Germans had greeted them with a hail of shells and there had been many victims.

ANZIO-NETTUNO BEACH HEAD

But this time they were able to land on the beach without a single shot being fired. (The spot was marked in yellow on the map of the Rangers and paratroops, between Anzio and Nettuno, while the green and red marks at the right, marked the landing- point of Truscott's infantry). Had the Germans adopted the Japanese technique, which allowed the first wave to come in, before opening fire?

But then the second and third waves arrived, also without meeting any obstacle. All of a sudden, as the sky began to lighten, there was the flare of an enemy battery, which fired few shells. Then it was silent for good, hit by a shot from one of the cruisers. It was at this point, somewhere in the "green" or "yellow" or "red" areas of the English sector, that Vaughan-Thomas landed with his portable recorder. His only concern was to avoid walking outside the white tapes which were stretched out like walkway between the minefields. He began to record the first disc with these words: "The dawn is fine and chill, and not an enemy in sight!". Also a little detachment, mostly Italian-Americans, Mexican-Americans, belonging to the Office of Strategic Service had landed by the old Sangallo Fortress whose owner Prince Barberini had also been evacuated from Nettuno. Their task was, as Louis Michielini recalled: "Infiltrate into

Germans lines by dressing civilian clothes and report to Fifth Army headquarters".

How was it possible? Churchill, from the military point of view, gave a convincing explanation of the easy approach, saying that the activities of the air force had been of great help: "Our heavy attacks on enemy airfields, and especially at Perugia, the German air reconnaissance base, kept many of their aircraft grounded". (Churchill, *Op. cit.* p. 425).

But what counted most of all was the sacrifice imposed on the Fifth Army which had had to resume the attack along the Garigliano river and around Cassino in the first in January, and which was beaten back with great loss of life.

According to Churchill the aim was to draw the attention and the reserve troops of the enemy away from the area chosen for the landing. This was achieved, but at a very high price: in that attack, which was so insistent that it seemed to be aimed at both shattering the defenses and carrying General Clark to a rapid reunion with the units of the 6th Corps, once this landed at Anzio-Nettuno, the 36th US Division, all of them Texas youths, found itself exposed to the fire of the German artillery on the banks of the Rapido, and during the crossing. There was no way of escape: 1681 men died in what the correspondents, in anger as well in sorrow, described as "the bigger disaster to American arms since Pearl Harbor".

In a reprimand which spared Clark no offence, The Texans demanded an enquiry into his conduct at the end of the war. Naturally, he was vindicated. "He had no option but to order the attack if the main front was to full fill its task of holding the enemy while the Anzio end run was in the making. The easy with which the Beachhead forces landed owed a great deal to the sacrifices of the Texan and other division around Cassino". (Vaughan-Thomas, *Op. cit.*, p. 41).

However, this was not all. When we look closely at the conduct of Field-Marshall von Kesserling, the Commander in Chief of all the German forces in Italy, we find another incredible fact. He had always feared a landing behind the Gustav Line, and had been forced, as we have seen, to leave his defenses weak because of the costly assault of the Fifth Army. It is also true that earlier on, looking out for the likeliest spots along the coast for amphibious operations, Kesserling himself had localized five (La Spezia, Viareggio, Livorno, Civitavecchia, Anzio), directing his thoughts towards the north of Rome. The same happened in the case of D-Day in Normandy. When the war had reached its final stage and all Germany was expecting a blow to come from the sea, the specialists in "blitzkrieg" again showed themselves to be unprepared in terms of insight and imagination. They had massed their divisions at the Pas de Calais, and were convinced that the deep sea-bed and the supposed lack of port facilities would make a landing in Normandy impossible; they never dreamed of the solution of prefabricated artificial landing-stages which the Allies used.

Field-Marshall von Rundstedt and Rommel, to whom the guardian of the Atlantic defenses had been entrusted, put the blame on mistaken signals from the secret services. In fact, the Anglo-Americans had taken the lead in the war of espionage as well. But in the case of Kesserling what happened was either a matter of ignorance or of enemy intelligence. His Chief of Staff Siegfried Westphal, testified: "On January 21st Admiral Canaris, Chief of the German Intelligence, visited Army Group headquarters, where he was pressed to communicate any information he might have about the enemy intentions in regard to a landing in particular we wanted to know about the positions of aircraft-carriers, battleships, and landing-crafts. Canaris was unable to give us any details, but thought that there was no need to fear a new landing in the next future. This was certainly his view. Not only the reconnaissance, but also the

German counter-espionage, was almost completely out of action at this time. A few hours after the departure of Canaris the enemy landed at Anzio". (Westphal, *Heer in Fesseln*, p. 240).

Was it, then, this "007" who betrayed Kesserling, inducing him to suspend the state of alarm in Anzio and Nettuno, and send all his soldiers to bed? The most faithful loyalist in the Third Reich suspected this especially when they were faced with proofs that some of the Admiral's closest collaborators had tried more than once to make approaches to the English. The SS arrested him in July 1944, after the failed attempt on Hitler's life. A few months later, without a regular trial, Wilhelm Canaris was condemned to be strangled: the executioner killed him slowly with a length of telephone wire around his neck.

THE GERMAN OCCUPATION

Where were the people of Nettuno and Anzio, and how were they living their lives amid all this? For anyone who seeks to come close to them and find out now about their story before the Americans came up from the shore, the picture is a confused one, and the colors are no longer those of the sea. In the background are the ruins of Italy abandoned since the 8th September, and here, right in front of us is the glaring unreal light of the desert towns. The Medieval town, the walkway surrounding the walls, the tamarisks on the seafront, the façade of the town hall with its small tower, the clock and shield under the cornice, Via Romana, the Caffè della Posta and further on, the Sangallo Fortress, in Nettuno; the Novel Art building of the Casino, the dockyard, the villas Albani and Aldobrandini, the pier of the harbor and Piazza Pia, in Anzio, all now looked like the skeletal Astura Tower and Nero's villa, paralyzed forever. From the day the occupation began, the Germans had set up their high command in the old building of the military Garrison in Piazza Mazzini.

The Garrison building, completed in 1902, had always housed the officers of the Italian Artillery School. They continue their activities today in the old shooting range beyond the Scacciapensieri skyscraper.

In fact, the shooting range had reached his 120 years, since it was started on 1st July 1888. Even with the advent of peace it hasn't been without its troubleshooters, as it has been the scene of pacifist demonstrations and demands for the reopening to the public of the stretch of coast cut off by the military restricted zone. There has so far been no change, however. The officers' residence has been moved to a building inside the firing area and Nettuno has had to get used to living with the booming of the guns and while the windows of the houses shudder thus doesn't help much in trying to forget the continuous gunfire of the landing. On the other hand it is only fair to take account of the interest of the many families who derive their living from it; and perhaps it should be admitted here that, without military barriers and once the polygon ceased to fire its guns and bar our boats from access to this little paradise, it will be hard to preserve from relentless advance of the concrete jungle that clear stretch of sea from Cretarossa to Valmontorio, with its Robinson Crusoe appeal to many of us.

To go back to the German occupation. They placed an anti-tank gun at the corner of the little Porfiri house and they pointed it directly at the walls of

ANZIO-NETTUNO BEACH HEAD

the Garrison building, ordering the Italian officers by megaphone to come out with their hands above their heads. The Commander, Colonel Bruno Toscano, replied: "Give me time to get the women and children out, and then do whatever you want". This happened a little after seven in the morning of 9th September, when another German unit, after marching on the little slope of Via St. Barbara, had already been directing its arms against the Piave Barracks for two hours. They were holding the barracks under threat of machine-gun fire from the terraces around. At the same time in Rome, three black cars surreptitiously left the Quirinale, not through the main door but through one of the side doors of the Ministry of War in Via XX Settembre. This was the flight of the King Victor Emmanuel III, with Marshall Badoglio, after the signing of the Armistice with the Anglo-American forces. They arrived safely at Pescara, and embarked in a corvette, which conveyed them equally safely to the port of Brindisi. And the Italians? They were left to try to deal with the Germans as best they could.

At Nettuno and Anzio, they did what they could. The small anti-tank gun in Piazza Mazzini, in Nettuno, from which three shots were fired that which direct hits on the first floor of the Garrison building, acted like a spark on the people of

Nettuno. It is no coincidence that the picture of this gun, escorted by two sentries, has been chosen for the cover of the only book which managed to bring together the reminiscences of the ordinary people who, for three days, had shown themselves capable of defending their own freedom while the radio news broadcasts never ceased giving the list of towns in Lazio that had surrendered.

Several Garrison officers who had been requested to come and fetch a safe-conduct, were instead rounded up and pushed into lorries, to begin their voyage with hope to the concentration camps; others, after finding themselves with their backs to the wall, succeeded in joining forces with the locals who had also rebelled against the sacking of their shops. To those who asked to be paid, the Germans replied with two words (in Italian): «Charge it to Badoglio». Colonel Toscano, who was under house arrest, sneaked out through the garden and joined the soldiers and civilians who had built barricades at the Sangallo fortress and the Belvedere.

As well as the Piave Barracks (assigned after the war to the School for NCO's of the security forces), and the Tofano Barracks inside the shooting range, there was also the Donati Barracks at Nettuno. It was a military complex of which only one small building has remained intact, in the area still waiting for a project of usage, near the present vegetable and fruit market. The Donati Barracks was the arsenal from which the people of Nettuno got most of their arms.

The revolt had begun in Piazza Mazzini. Above the wide sidewalk which form a kind of atrium to Viale Matteotti before the arch in Via del Quartiere, and is the meeting place for the people of Nettuno and holidaymakers for the evening stroll towards St. Rocco, they have put a marble plaque. It is on a kind of smoothed-off corner which appears to be the fortified flank or buttress of the outermost wall of the old walled town. You really need to hunt for this plaque, raising your eyes above the neon sign of the Bar Volpi. It is far from conspicuous; indeed it's quite hard to see. Even the inscription, without any signature, and devoid of superlatives, is the opposite of vainglorious: «in this square, on the initiative of number of brave-spirited citizens, the people of Nettuno rose against the Nazi-fascist on the 8th, 9th and 10th September 1943».

The date is incorrect, since the insurrection actually started on the 9th. These brave-spirited people, apart from the second lieutenant of the tank corps who led them, and one or two others who had escaped from the chaos of military disintegration thanks to a leave, had never handled a weapon. They were boys, like Marcello Simeoni who was hardly seventeen years old.

However, the motive force which galvanized them was the shout from someone who was old enough to be their father, Giuseppe Ottolini, the *'Commendatore'*, another personage in the gallery of important members of the Nettuno community. His name is linked to the building of the skyscraper and the residential district of Scacciapensieri. Certainly, that for those who still remember the regular line of the coast as it once was, and who find the skyscraper a great eyesore. He has earned a great deal more honor from the words which he used to inspire the young men at that time: "People of Nettuno. Let's go and fight!".

From Piazza Mazzini to the Donati Barracks, abandoned by the military, it was a short hop. Out came everything, and the hungry people also joined in. The rebels provided themselves with sub-machine guns, rifles and hand grenades. They also found a heavy machine-gun, which however jammed. They repaired it in the photography workshop of the Barattoni brothers. Only one of them really knew how to handle it, Costantino Cestarelli. He lived in Via dello Steccato, on the raised walkway of the old town. He had come back from the front, and his experience enabled him to instruct the boys of Piazza Mazzini how to fire it. This, however, didn't prevent a burst of fire escaping from the machine-gun while it was being

ANZIO-NETTUNO BEACH HEAD

tested, which broke the main electric cable and left the town in darkness for quite a few hours.

It was difficult to track down Costantino and find out the names of his companions. More than one of them has died: Lorenzo Lucci, known as "Poppetto", Giuseppe Bruzzi the inspector from Ansaldo, Umberto Mastrogirolamo, known as "Gazzone", and Giuseppe Roveri the town electrician. These were the ones that Costantino spoke about most. He himself has left the old town and gone to live in the country between the village of Tre Cancelli and the big fountain of the Seccia (today without water). He built the house there himself and has a fair piece of land to go with it, with a vineyard and a garden as well as a hen run. He also talked about Mario Trippa, another of those who instructed the boys, and of Angelo Simone, who took such great care of the machine-gun that his finger never left the trigger, so afraid was he that he would jam again; and of the youngest Marcello Simeoni who, having positioned himself with a machine-gun on the terrace of the Carabinieri Barracks, in Via St. Maria, overturned a side-car with two Germans in it. "Don't try to make us sound like heroes", he advised us. "We didn't do anything out of the ordinary. Earlier on they had told us that an armored column was moving forward from Amzio

Colonia, so we knew how impotent we were. But just for a moment we felt we were really a proper army, thanks to Angelo Lauri".

He was the second-lieutenant of the tank corps. Many years after the war it was possible to meet him in the port, where he had a nautical office. He had never stopped working, moving on from the farm of Acciarella to the building industry, and then on to boats and boating. On three successive occasions, in the municipal elections of 1960, 1965 and 1970, the people of Nettuno voted him into office. In the first five years he was Councilor in Charge of Sport and Public Works, and he played a major role in the building of the municipal stadium which, with the football and baseball fields and tennis court, the skating rink, athletic tracks, changing rooms, rostrum and caretaker's house, cost altogether 64 million lire.

Angelo had been promoted to second-lieutenant in Bologna, with the 3rd Armored Regiment, after having passed the training courses for NCO's and Officers. As he came tenth in the course, he had a right to select his duty station. He chose Rome. Thus he arrived, in the month preceding the Armistice, at the barracks of the 4th Regiment in Via Tiburtina. He could get to Nettuno in an hour by train. In order to take up a position in Piazza Mazzini from his own house (where on the evening of the 8th September he had felt as he were a deserter) all he had to do was go down the steps.

His idea, naturally, was bound to be connected with tanks. Apart from refusing to hand over his pistol to the Germans, his pride would not let him take off his uniform, the summer one, with shorts and long socks. It was this, rather than his rank, which placed him at the head of his fellow-citizen. He told us: "In the Donati Barracks the first steps were taken. Then I took with me a small group of friends, and we went to the shooting range, where the tanks were. We rendered them unusable by taking away the breech-blocks of the cannons and the fuel injection pumps of the engines. The Germans could never use them again. But we left one intact for our own use. It was an M13. A medium sized tank of 13 tons. I took the driving seat, while two or three others were posted at the guns and the machine-guns. That was how we returned to Mazzini square, and the noise of the tracks fired our enthusiasm".

After the tank, the people of Nettuno were reinforced by a small detachment of infantry from Fogliano. But their greatest comfort came from the courage of some of the soldiers of the Piave Barracks. The Germans had induced the commander of the barracks to surrender, and there was nothing left for him to do but gather his men in the courtyard. He told them that there was no hope of resistance, and they must lay down their arms. Not all of them obeyed his order. While the gate was being opened to the German trucks, which already knew where they had to go, the hand of an artilleryman who had climbed in from outside hurled a grenade from the top of a wall, and this was the signal for revolt. The Germans were hounded out. As they went back down Via St. Barbara, they couldn't avoid a clash with those who had dug themselves in at the Sangallo Fortress, and they came for worse.

Nettuno was in the hands of its own people. The most popular footballer of the period, Silvio Piola, the Lazio centre-forward since 1934, had taken up his place on the barricades. He too was in uniform; although he was already thirty years old, he had been called up and assigned as an artilleryman to the Macao Barracks in Rome. But he had found time to pay a short visit to Anzio and Nettuno, where he liked to indulge his passion for hunting and fishing. It would be hard to forget how the athlete, nearing his fortieth year, made a vigorous comeback to the blue shirts in 1952 for the drawn match between Italy and England at Florence. But even more than the memory of his back-kicks and his goals, he has left the people of Nettuno the example of a brave Italian who participated in their battle. Mario Trippa recalls: "With Piola we went with a lorry to the Piave Barracks, where we loaded arms and foodstuff that we distributed to everyone, and then we went with the others to the Sangallo fortress and succeeded in attacking a bus load of Germans".

It was only a matter of improvised resistance by an isolated and unarmed small town to a power which had crushed Europe beneath its heel. Even so, we needed that gesture as does the reassertion of every right. After having given the impression of retreating and going off towards Campoleone, the Germans came back with large numbers.

There was also a Stukas attack; the planes showered bombs on Viale Mencacci. The bombardment didn't spare the roofs of Nettuno, and above all, part of the H. Goering Armored Division headed for Cassino was detached to Anzio and then to Villa Borghese and Piazza Mazzini.

The end of the resistance was achieved by negotiations, in which the Germans promised that there would be no reprisals against the civilians population or against the military. But in practice they could impose their own conditions, threatening the destruction of the town. On the morning of 12th September, in front of Valery's shop, the Commissioner of the Police Pietro Li Voti and a German Officer with a megaphone told the boys of Piazza Mazzini that there was nothing else to be done. A little later, Colonel Toscano was forced to call together the soldiers of the Piave Barracks and persuade them to surrender, while a small van carrying the white flag moved through the streets of Nettuno. It was midday.

Despite the promises, the reprisals were heavy. These are the darkest days of all, the days of manhunts, deportations, shooting in a nape of the neck. They should, however, be re-read with the awareness of who was responsible and, above all, with those sentiments that led, in the post-war period, to the twinning of Nettuno with the German town of Traunreut. Our friends in Bavaria welcome us with open arms to their ultra-modern town (which grew up sixty years ago at the very point where Hitler kept hidden in the shadow of the woods one of the biggest explosive dumps of his whole army) and repay us with a visit every year. It begins with their participation in the procession of the first Saturday in May when the Madonna of Grace is brought out from St. Rocco's church for the customary journey to St. Giovanni's church. They also stay on with us to enjoy the sea-bathing during the hot summer months. These friends from Traunreut are the real represent-tatives, for us, of the freedom and peace purchased at the expense of so much bloodshed.

The wall which runs down from Piazza Mazzini to the beach, pock-marked by the volleys which put an end to the lives of so many martyrs, is the symbol of all that resistance to Nazi-fascism. The executions were something to be carried out quickly, with no preliminaries. A boy from Armellino area, found with a pair of pliers in his hand to repair the wire of his cattle enclosure, and taken by the Germans for a saboteur (the telephone cable of their camp a few yards away had been cut), was forced aboard a side-car and taken to headquarters. They left him outside for a few minutes in the custody of the guards. Just long enough for a sergeant and four soldiers to go in and out. Then they took him again and dragged him to the wall, made him turn his head, and the sergeant killed him with three shots from his pistol, in the presence of the women who were standing in line waiting for the paper permission to be in town.

That sergeant had no doubt that he had done his duty, as he believed the discipline of the Wehrmacht and martial law regulations demanded of him. The day after, he went to Alfonso Bernardini's bakery in Via Cavour (still a bakery today, under the name of Paoloni), where he used to get a few rolls of bread underhand. One of the bakers, Dante Castaldi, asked him whether he didn't feel some remorse for what happened to the boy, and he was amazed. "Why ever should I? In fact, I did it in a such a way that he didn't suffer".

AT THE PORT OF ANZIO

Succeeded in driving the Germans out of the Piave barracks, at 10.30 sergeant Carlo Colombi, together with sergeant Puzzi, a university student, who was a native of Salerno, took the road to Anzio. Colombi had come to Anzio from Genoa and he had married a woman from Anzio, Anna Giacomelli. They lived in Via del Porto Neroniano, 71. It can be assigned in the Anzio uprising (where relations with the Germans had become rather tense even before 8th September, following the killing of Anna Minghiacchi, known as Nannina, to whom is dedicated a street in Anzio, struck on July 18th in the restaurant of her father in via XX Settembre from the revolver of a drunken soldier who claimed more wine after the closure of the store), the role that Lauri had in Nettuno. "When I reached my wife", said Colombi, "I realized that the Germans were aiming to seize the port. Two of their side-cars came and went, and in the evening they ended up strafing the people on the dock. There were wounded, even a dead man, I think, amid the fragments of the windows of two or three shops. An act of terrorism to disperse us. That night, instead, we gathered in the air raid shelters and there we prepared a plan for the next day". At dawn on September 10th, then, thirty or so rebels went to fight: civilians and soldiers, among whom Colombi remembered the Carboni's brothers, who had their family in Alexandria, Egypt, sergeant Villotta, plus an agent. of Polizia Africa Italiana (Italian African Police), Michele Gallo, who was also married to a women of Anzio. In the harbor there were fishing boats, used for dredging mines and for laying them. They belonged to the Biondi's brothers. Heavy fishing machine guns and some light machine guns Breda 38 were taken from the fishing boats. Colombi arranged them on the roof of his house in Via del Porto Neroniano and in the neighboring house of Criscuolo, and from there, the harbor and the western Riviera were under fire.

On the ground was used an old British cannon of World War I, an Amstrong 75 / 27, used to defend the port. It was moved from where there is today the restaurant "Da Romolo - Al porto" and placed at the entrance of Via del Porto Innocenziano, to prevent the access of the Germans to Piazza Pia.

That cannon, around eleven, gave way to hostileties, targeting an artillery truck that was coming down from via Aldobrandini, better known then as the road of the Icehouse. The vehicle was hit. The Germans, thrown to the ground, took care to collect the injured and bring them at the military hospital. Not all, though. Some of them climbed the church's bell tower and for a while could act like snipers. Among the victims Raffaele Palomba, a fisherman, father of eleven children, who was part of the group of rebels led by Colombi and who, hit at midday by a dum-dum bullet, died in the evening at the military hospital, Claudio Paolini, fell the next day in a clash with the Germans at the Zanardelli Riviera, Felice Puddu, Sergio Ghiardini, Lucillo Galbio and Davide Alessandrelli.

For two days, the port of Anzio remained in the hands of the people of Anzio, as Nettuno was in the hands of the Nettuno people. In those days many civilian, anyhow, were killed in action. Amongst them Palomba and Paolini from Anzio. To them as well the city dedicated a square and a street.

In divided Italy, the ferocity of the war was made worse by the cowardly treachery of informers. Anti-fascists, forced to take to the countryside with their families, had also to be on constant guard against traps. Mario De Franceschi (the first democratically elected mayor of Nettuno after the war, in 1946) fell into one of them. He was not one of those who knew nothing about their baits. However, when they told him that it was rumored that his house already commandeered and turned upside down, had been left open for anyone to enter, he couldn't resist. The moment he put his nose inside the old town again, as soon as he went through the Baluardo Arch, he found a German colonel waiting for him.

He could not but feel it was the end. In Piazza Mazzini, some other unfortunates, probably arested in the surrounding villages, were already standing with their backs to the wall of death. It seemed to De Franceschi that he didn't know anyone there. But then, among the Germans who were preparing to interrogate him, he recognized a woman, Mrs Tortora. She was a strange woman of about sixty, aloof, untidy and badly dressed, with her stockings downs around her knees: the embodiment of slovenliness. It was said that she had moved to Nettuno to be near her daughter and son-in-law (an artillery sergeant who had been employed in at an anti-aircraft battery until the 8th September). De Franceschi had already met her in the old town, and had carried away an impression that she was something of a phenomenon because he had heard her speak six different languages. So he caught her eyes and she persuaded the German colonel to release him.

No one ever knew the name of this odd, slovenly woman. Was it Anna? Giulia? Argea? De Franceschi, for his part, had every reason to believe that she was more than just a simple interpreter for the Germans. After the landing, when the jeep of the Italo-American lieutenant De Rubeis stopped in front of her house at the end of Via Vittorio Veneto, and everyone expected to see her come out in handcuffs, they found instead that the lieutenant had gone there to thank her for the services rendered to the Allies; she was in fact a secret agent, sent to Nettuno from Turkey.

The Germans always avoided setting foot in the woods, where the majority of the young people, threatened by the round-ups were hiding. They roamed about during the day, but went to ground at night. Public order, presumably the task of those 'Carabinieri' and customs or Police officers who still held their posts, ended up being kept by the few civic policemen on duty at the time. Their main job was to ensure the smooth functioning of what was then a most vital service: the distribution of rationed food supplies.

The entire force of civic policemen (known as municipal guards or agents) consisted of 10 elements: 5 from Nettuno and 5 from Anzio, as decreed by the joint municipal administration of Nettunia. Having to be central, they has aptly chosen the white building on the Zanardelli Riviera, named 'Paradiso', as its headquarters. The force was headed by Giovanni Simeoni. We still have on file Giovanni's sorrowful letter of 7 January 1944 to Nettuno's prefect, Commissioner

Ignazio De Matteis, from which we can glean the dreadful adversities faced by the people of Nettuno who, on top of everything else, had to put up with the speculations of individuals of no scruples who took advantage of the situation to increase their riches.

In this regard Nettuno had its share of sharks. As we shall see, it was Giovanni Simeoni who denounced their misdeeds. His subordinates, besides the ones from Anzio who operated under direct jurisdiction of Brigadier Giulio Novara, included his fellow-citizens Ligorio Ricci, Bruno Belleudi, Rodrigo Taurelli and Fernando De Franceschi (the latter had been recalled for military service). After the 8th of September, Giovanni had evacuated with his family to Zucchetti area by the orders of De Matteis, who had requested and obtained from the Germans that they allow only one policeman to be on duty in each city.

Thus begins the adventure of Ligorio Ricci, a good fellow, forced to remain in uniform and to turn himself into a sort of the facto sheriff, with broad belt, revolver in its holster and armband with 'Kriminal Polizie' written on it. He was the one who roamed around Nettuno from curfew to dawn, acting like the boss, but taking great care not to notice the shadows that sometimes appeared in the doorways.

The majority of people in Nettuno had not complied immediately with the evacuation order, first issued on 23rd September 1943. The order was to leave their homes and to keep more than five kilometers away from the coast. Thousands of people had taken refuge elsewhere, mostly in Rome. The others were too deeply attached to their land. Their vineyards, their gardens and the countryside which gave them their only sense of freedom, and preferred to take risks.

Even though so near, the war seemed far away, and as long as the bombs were not raining down from the Flying Fortress (the first Allied air attack took place on 19th October), it was still possible to keep up the illusion that it 'couldn't touch us'. Only the very old, fatalistic, had made their decision: here we were born and here we will die.

The Germans used men of all ages to plant mines, and also enlisted the women to clean their offices and peel potatoes. And so the life of stray dogs began: days in the countryside and nights in the cellars and caves, which, until the liberation of Rome, was the lot of the people of Nettuno and Anzio (just a handful, in the end) who had not said goodbye to their town. The 'sheriff', we may add, was really on their side, and knew how to close an eye. He also did what he could to avoid leaving them without food, since the peasants couldn't scrape anything together any longer, and not everyone could afford the black market. Some of the mothers, by making the hazardous journey to Rome, had managed to get some oil for the pan and a few kilos of pasta, in exchange for sheets and gold earrings.

Even salt had vanished, and the experiment of cooking with sea-water was an immediate failure, an inedible mess. Flour for bread, rationed like all other foodstuffs but sill the only one not to have disappeared all together, was beginning to run out, partly because the Germans were commandeering it.

At the Jannozzi mill in Via Sangallo, they no longer knew where the grain would come from. Ligorio Ricci then had a bright idea worthy of a medal. Armed with his 'Kriminal Polizie' armband, he took a cart to the depot in Via Romana (the building now occupied by a coffee shop) and without hesitation got Angelo Zecchinelli, the guard, to hand over to him the sacks of about 400 quintals of grain which the Wehrmacht had confiscated for its own use. The Germans were never to see that grain again. After dividing it into two equal parts, Ligorio used it to supply the four bakeries in Nettuno and the four in Anzio which had finished up their supplies. After this, if he didn't vanish, he was going to be roasted. On 10th December, Andrea Mariola and a Commissioner of the Police, Cardinali, helped him to get away to a hiding place in his brother-in-law's at Soriano del Cimino. Having made himself scarce in this way, he got a fine present in exchange: he was not able to make use of the subsidy normally paid to evacuees!

In the meantime, on 26th November, Giovanni Simeoni had again taken up his post, on his own initiative. Once he found out that the Germans had cleaned out his Piazza Colonna home, he showed up at their command. Although he was of course unable to recover the stolen items, he was least given the symbolic assignment of investigating into the affair. He took full advantage of his assignment, putting the law between the people of Nettuno and the sharks. With his agents he checked prices (bread Lit. 5 per kg; pasta Lit. 5; sugar Lit. 20; salt Lit. 6; jam Lit. 25; tomato conserve Lit. 18; beef Lit. 50; soap Lit. 5 per bar), punished all rationing violations and issued a whole bunch of fines.

In the end however, 15 days before the landing, he was forced to bitterly admit in his letter to De Matteis that the sharks had proven stronger than he: "...It is impossible to control the gluttony of those who are starving the population. The merchants these days are doing by filching the goods to sell them at higher prices".

Not even the greatly venerated Madonna of Grace, the patron of Nettuno, could evoid exile. Mindful of the adventure which had driven her from long-distant Ipswich in England to the shores of St. Rocco, she cannot have been the least frightened by the new journey which was imposed on her on the morning of the 6th December, after having spent the night in a railway carriage in the Villa Borghese tunnel. In any case, of all the her children, only a handful remained. (Nettuno then had about twelve thousand inhabitants and Anzio eight thousands – today they count one hundred thousand all together). The Germans had had to repeat the evacuation order on 2nd October and, seeing that it was still resisted, they decreed ten days later that anyone discovered in town or its vicinity would be shot.

One of the clergy's major worries concerned the holy statue. Don Nicola De Franceschi, the elderly archpriest, and Don Angelo Mariola, the parish vicar, Don Vincenzo Cerri and Don Pietro Bürge had all had to yield to the evacuation injunction and had had to shut St. Giovanni's Church. Don Vincenzo, looking out from the belfry in the days following the Armistice, could hear the Germans' bullets whistling all around him. He left for Piscina Cardillo. Only Don Angelo stayed in town, and it was left to him to carry the wooden statue to safety. It was no joke. With all divine allowances, it was still a case of smuggling something which couldn't exactly be slipped into a pocket like a small item. Two friars, Vincenzo and Gabriele, furtively moved the Madonna on the only train (a slow one), which kept open the link between Nettuno/Anzio and Rome. Don Angelo himself, together with Gabriele, deposited her in the Oratory of the Scala Sancta at the Lateran, from where it was afterwards transferred to the basilica of Saints John and Paul on the Coelian Hill, and displayed there for devotion.

The whistle and clatter of the train, which followed the old line through Cecchina, seemed to be the last sign of life in Nettuno and Anzio until the landing. Even the town council officers had had to be evacuated, and then transferred to the capital, the name of Nettunia was retained, and the offices were established in a building on the Via delle Terme di Diocleziano only ten days before the arrival of the Allies. The post office, which had also been moved to Rome, consisted of a counter in Via della Vite, 113.

This was basically the bureaucratic structure. However, the Nettunia administration, personified by Commissioner De Matteis, as he wrote, had already takes to its heels as early as 24th September, relying for its registry and rationing service on the four employers left: Mario Eufemi, Angelo Catanzani and the Ludovisi sisters, Caterina and Ada. The latter, whose task was to obtain the bread-ration cards in Via dei Cerchi in Rome, needed to say her prayers more than the others, since there was no other way of getting there than by train, constantly the target of planes that swooped down to machine-gun it.

Eufemi acted as their supervisor, partly for the skill he had demonstrated in forging German traffic permits and getting more than one Nettuno lorry back on the road. Now, together with Angelo, Caterina and Ada, he was forced to do a mobile job, to trace the townspeople who had been driven from the coast.

These people were crowded into farm-houses, huts, cattle-sheds and so on from the area of Seccia, Cioccati, Zucchetti, Piscina Cardillo and Tre Cancelli, as far as Le Ferriere. But the majority of the people of Nettuno, like the people of Anzio, had to rummage among the trash in order to survive. Along the shore of Anzio Colonia, outside the St. Barbara Barracks, there were prefabricated huts made out of wood and pressed cardboard. They had served as a kind of den for the Fascist

militia in the period when they were assigned to guards the shores. They were just big boxed, full of cracks. It was, however possible to put in a table and still stretch out on a pallet. The Germans allowed the evacuees to load them on to carts and carry them away, as in Biblical exodus.
Their promised land, though, was nothing more than a sub-district of Nettuno. They reached it by taking the road to Velletri and turning at Cadolino. On the higher ground, beyond the cork woods and the flat-lands which are covered with watermelons in the summer, is the pine-wood of the Campana. Tourism has now bestowed the name of Isola Verde on it, and it has a campsite with all facilities for caravans. This was where the people of Nettuno and Anzio, no longer like cat and dog to each other, as their long-standing rivalry had previously decreed, camped to wait for the worst to pass, amid the chilly cardboard walls left behind by the militia.
The Campana was, however, the destination of the four foot-travelers from the Town Hall who arrived with their tomes and their files under their arms. There was also another willing character, 'Nanni' Giovanni Serra, to give them a hand. But where could they set up their 'office'? On the road, which was really no more than a cart-truck, just before the descent to the Sambuco creek, there was one of

the many Borghese family farm. It is still standing, with its external staircase, despite the war and the passage of time, over beyond the bushes. The factor was still living there with his family, which must have been very numerous, since Eufemi, Ada, Angelo and Caterina, although warmly welcomed with their assistant, were nevertheless relegated with a table and a few chairs to the henhouse (which the fowl, for obvious reasons of prevailing hunger, had already vacated).

Now that the 'sheriff' had gone, the night was more night than ever. The only company left to the God Neptune at that time in the Market Place was the sound of the low voices of the bakers, when they met near his fountain on their way to prepare the dough. Apart from the Bernardini bakery in Via Cavour, that of Margherita Ricci in Via Cattaneo (then called Via Conte di Torino), was still operating. One of the severest air bombardments, halfway through December, had put the Palazzetti bakery in Piazza Mazzini out of action, and that of Porfirio Ottolini on the corner of Via St. Maria had also been forced to close down. However, in the toughest period of the German occupation, when the heart of Nettuno and Anzio was in the Campana, the evacuees were provided with a bit of comfort (indeed even with a touch of festivity) by the figure of Margherita, tall and smiling, with her raven colored hair, as she came with her cart to bring them bread. They also received bread from Castore and Alessandro Marigliani whose father, Clemente, had transferred his bakery from Anzio to a vineyard at Miglioramento, on the Via della Cannuccia.

Taking into account the presence of the bakers, we can calculate the number of townspeople who remained in Nettuno until the end as roughly thirty. Apart from the collaborators (some of them quite innocent, in fact, like the barber who had to rush off every morning and shave them) the Germans could not refuse permits to the electricians Salvatore Bertolini and Vincenzo Roveri, to the plumber Umberto Graziosi, or finally to the Donatis who owned the last villa in Via Romana, at the far end. The villa was in fact commandeered as a hostel for the officers, but the Donatis, set up house in a nearby cave, they managed to get something out of the Germans, however, thank to Ciro and Pietro, both of whom were doctors. They asked to be allowed to care for the wounded, and the infirm, who were in desperate straits and aware of their worst problem: the lack of medicine and proper cures.

The military sanatorium at Anzio was open to the civilians population but the problem for the evacuees was how to get there, eluding the

Germans' constantly leveled guns? The initiative and the sacrifices of few people provided a remedy. One of the streets of Nettuno in the new district of Cretarossa had been dedicated to 'Sister Eletta del Rosario' in the world born as Angela Barattieri. She had begun as a young nun in the wards of the Orsenigo hospital and for fifty years she had given consolation to troubled souls. She was a nurse who, in the end, knew as much as a leading specialist, and undoubtedly she was a saint. Her miracles, like carrying out in a hut an operation which would normally have required the full facilities of an operating theatre, were witnessed by the people of Nettuno and Anzio driven from home.

Along with S ister Eletta, we should also mention Vincenzo Monti, the municipal doctor. He joined the refugees, sheltering in a hut near Piscina Cardillo. Ciro and Pietro Donati, on the other hand, were allowed to set up an infirmary on the first floor of their villa. One of their niece, Fernanda Loffredi, the daugther of Melania, taught many of Nettuno's children to read and write in the post-war years. She had never ceased to think that some of those children may well have been there thanks to her uncles, who also succeeded in making room in their infirmary for those who were about to give birth.

In those conditions, the picture of childbirth, so it seemed, no longer had that heavenly glow, the glow apparent in the actions, the gentleness of old women sitting outside their houses in the old town on summer evenings, knitting baby clothes for their recently married daughters. How could they remember these things in the freezing cold of the camps, in those wood and cardboard cells where everything they possessed was hung on a nail? And could they really look forward to a wailing cry between the groans of those in labor when they sank to the ground in resignation, as though they could not survive their ordeal?

None of them, however, got forgotten. The maternal instinct exist also in the way every woman hurries to the aid of another in the act which is their own most intimate preserve. 'Sora Bianca' and 'Sora Ada' midwives from Nettuno and Anzio, called on from far away and managing to be here, there and everywhere among the evacuees, demonstrated that despite everything it was still possible to come into the world.

ANZIO-NETTUNO BEACH HEAD

This cartoon from the Daily Express, gives an idea of the encircling operation that the expedition Corps of the Fifth Army, was to have carried out from Nettuno-Anzio, behind the strong German defense, known as the Gustav Line.

THE MIDWIVES IN ACTION

The first of these, Bianca Bellanti, whose married name was Amoretti, had moved from Florence to Nettuno in 1920. On September 8th, she had obtained a permit to move around freely wearing the Red Cross armband, and this enabled her to do often rescue operations, even among the men. They would managed to escape the German round-ups and deportations by passing themselves as husbands of unseen pregnant wives. Later on she too was forced to obey the evacuation order. She and her family took refuge in a farm between Borgo Montello and Le Ferriere, and she never parted with the little wooden box where she kept the instruments of her profession.

Not far away, in fact very near her house, was the hideout of Libera Ada Mantovani, married name Lucci, known as 'Sora Ada'. The place was however more suited to an acrobat's dexterity than the prudent steps of the midwife, it had been made out of a well. It still exist today, in the courtyard of the convent dedicated to St. Lucia Filippini, on the left hand side of the street which runs from the main square in Anzio to the station railway. The winch and the bucket-rope were in disuse, and one had to make use of iron supports embedded in the wall to go down to a depth of about thirty feet and reach two small tunnels, one opposite the other, in which a number of small beds were placed.

In this mole-hole 'Sora Ada' lived with her husband and children, and messengers from the Campana came to her there, frequently in the middle of the night on the most urgent missions. But when there was not even time to get to her or to 'Sora Bianca', that was the moment for the initiative and experience of those who had already been through a number of pregnancies. The most readily available of these was Perfetta Colaceci, or the widow Conti, known as 'the Midwife of the Ravenna district'. She was a peasant woman with the muscles and rough hands of a man and the wings of an angel. Her husband had been dead for more than ten years, and the whole burden of the household, the crops, the cattle, the four growing children, has fallen on her shoulder. She was bent with exhaustion, after hoeing the ground and pasturing the cattle from morning to night. And yet, apart from her courage she never lacked the strength to start off again across the fields under the bombs and force the war to make room for another human being, for when life become impossible it shoud be 'chastised by living it' as the poet Vincenzo Cardarelli recommended. (Cardarelli, *Poesie, Alla deriva – Poetry, To Drift*, p. 125).

To complete the list of benefactors, we should also mention Prince Stefano Borghese, known as Steno. When everything was falling apart. He at least kept alive the notion of a proper government which at that time did not even exist. For years, it seemed that the office of mayor (the 'Podestà' as the fascist regime chose to term it) had been abolished in Nettuno and Anzio; the towns had had to manage with officials of the Prefecture. This had already been the case back in 1935, and seven years later, the position was revived in the person of Ignazio De Matteis, whom we've already seen. Having retired to Rome, he at least had the merit of delegating Prince Borghese to represent him in loco. Even in misfortune, some fortune can appear. Lean, balding, a tiny bird compared with the German hawks, 'Steno' nevertheless knew how to make his presence felt. His firmness made it possible to save what could be saved.

It can be said finally. We are not now at the last hours, but at the last minutes, of the Nazi-fascist regime in Anzio-Nettuno. Only the bakers, however, were aware of the arrival of the Allies before the explosion of the rockets which preceded the landing by a few minutes; in fact it was one baker only, Orlando Castaldi, working away as he did every night at the yeast and the dough in Margherita Ricci's bakery. Everyone, including the war correspondents, has said that there was a strange silence on that night. But what can make a silence different from usual? Perhaps they perceived the pulsing, the heartbeats of the men who were crouching down and holding their breath? But no, Orlando felt something more substantial than that coming from the sea on that night.

He had been in Sicily, during the first Allied landings there, and now it seemed to him that the he could again sense and hear what he had sensed and heard then. For a moment he was still in doubt, while his workmates, his brother Marcello and Guglielmo Branella were holding out the pallets to take the first French rolls out of the oven. It was quarter to two in the morning. Orlando said: "Keep still a moment. Something's happening". Then taking Branella by the arm: "I can hear them; I can hear them... The Americans are coming! It's the same sound they made when Patton landed". He flung on his jacket and persuaded his workmates to pull the blinds down and leave, though he went first to warn his other brother Dante and his uncle Luigi who was working in the Bernardini bakery. They had hardly turned the corner of Via Cavour when the sky lit up, the earth trembled and they had the impression of being thrown into the air along with the houses.

The rest of the people of Nettuno-Anzio were unaware that anything had happened. Even those who were near the sea, the few who were sleeping in the towns, hardly awoke. They just turned over and went back to sleep, thinking it was only the normal bombardment. Don Steno at Villa Borghese was the only one to jump out of bed at the sound of the rockets. He put on his dressing-gown and watched from the small balcony off his bedroom. Perhaps he was the only spectator, among the tall pines, the ilexes and the palms, of that tidal wave sweeping over Anzio-Nettuno. However, one evacuee at Le Ferriere was still up and about. With his ear glued to the radio, he heard the message from Radio-London: "Cyril has arrived". It was the first news for Italy that the landing had taken place, but he didn't realize it.

ANZIO-NETTUNO BEACH HEAD

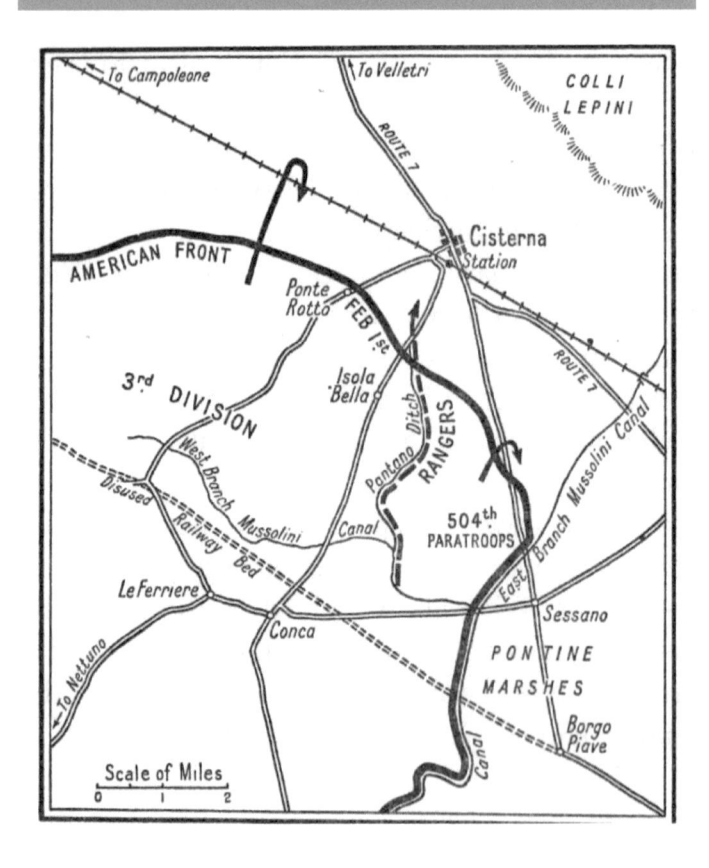

The attempt to break-out in the American sector, January 30th, 1944 was a failure from the start, even though they had preceded it by infiltrating the German lines with over 700 Rangers. In single file, like a snake, the Rangers had slipped through during the night almost to Cisterna Railway Station, only to find themselves, at dawn, surrounded by the Germans lying in wait. Only six survived.

ANZIO-NETTUNO BEACH HEAD

The Germans organized very fast and surrounded the beachhead in 48 hours.

ANZIO-NETTUNO BEACH HEAD

Field-Marshall Albert Kesserling, Commander-in-Chief South-West and Army Group C. After the war he recalled: "It would have been the Anglo-Americans doom to overextend themselves. I was quickly gathering my first five divisions to attack, the landing force was initially weak, only two divisions of infantry, and without armor. It was a half-measure as an offensive, that was the basis error".

ANZIO-NETTUNO BEACH HEAD

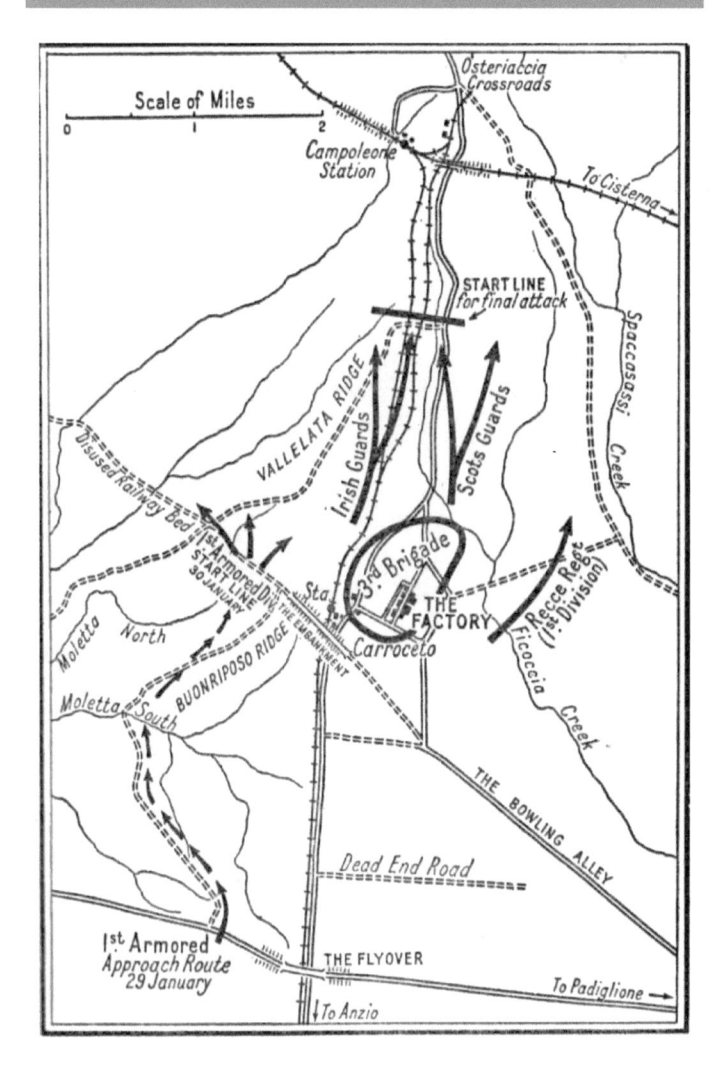

In the advance to Campoleone, 29th-30th January, 1944 all the British could do was to occupy Aprilia and a little beyond.

ANZIO-NETTUNO BEACH HEAD

"The German troops of the Reich have now launched their offensive on the Nettuno-Anzio front...". Thus began a German dispatch on February 10th, 1944. It was the lead-up to Operation Fishfang, the great offensive which Hitler himself set off 6 days later. After having recaptured Aprilia, they penetrated the Allied defense and broke through the line between Campo di Carne and the Padiglione tower.

THE CRISIS AND STALEMATE

The landing had succeeded. The only inconvenient had been to two British detachments who ran into mines in the neighborhood of Lido dei Pini. The port of Anzio was taken intact. After three hours the Allied could unload their armored cars and send out their reconnaissance patrols. Four bridges on the Moscarello (Mussolini) Canal were blown up to stave off the Panzers. By midday Lucas had disembarked over 35.000 men and innumerable vehicles between the area of Foce Verde and the Moletta Ditch. It Was a walkover with all due respect for those who had lost their lives. The coastal defense had been non-existent except for the mine-fields and a few unused pillboxes. With only one company of engineers on the spot and two battalions in the surrounding district, Kesserling was in effect unarmed. But the Allies, intent on consolidating their positions and waiting for two more divisions in arrive, gave him the opportunity to reorganize himself and block their advance. And so it happened that on the 30th January when Lucas felt secure enough to move on and take Cisterna and Campoleone, all that the British 1st Division could do was to occupy Aprilia and a little beyond. The American 3rd Division's attack was a failure from the start, even though they had preceded it by infiltrating the enemy lines with over 700 Rangers. In single files, like snakes, the Rangers had slipped through during the night almost to Cisterna only to find themselves, at dawn, surrounded by the Germans lying in wait. Only six survived.

THE MISSED OPPORTUNITY

Faced with an easy chance of scoring a goal, that of the open road to Rome, the Americans have been accused all through these years of missing the opportunity. The prosecution, to give some idea of the counter-blow which they received, demanded and obtained the condemnation of General Lucas, who was replaced in the field by his fellow-countryman Truscott a month after the landing. Even today he is still subjected to hoots and boos, like the centre-forward who missed an open goal. It would only have taken a little kick to put the ball in the net. Why did not the centre-forward Lucas not take the advantage? How can we avoid siding with the fans forced to watch the spectacle of their own team floundering, closed up in the penalty area?

The English in particular have dealt harshly with Lucas, convinced that because of his excessive caution he threw away what should then, and should still now, be considered one of Churchill's strategic masterpieces. But in the story of the missed goal, Lucas is in fact least to blame. Those who maintain that he had let the ball get away because he was not expecting it are quite wrong. There were surprises all around, and it seems quite credible that after having fired a left shot at Kesserling, it had rebounded against the Allies, who in turn were so astonished at the absence of the Germans that thay remained paralyzed. It could be that this is what happened in Lucas's case, who at 54 was treated as if he were an old dodderer, cautious and procrastinating to a higher degree even than Fabius Maximus. What made him hesitated to venture were the plans agreed with Alexander and Clark, rather than the fear of falling with his men into a non-existent trap, and also the dimensions of the expedition which could not in any way aspire on its own to the conquest of Rome.

Beginning with Churchill himself, the English have been unjust to Lucas. It is still said today that the mistake was to put someone in charge of the 6th Corps who was too cautious (but who, we should remember, had been called to replace his colleague General Dawley in Salerno because the latter was too imprudent). Even with a bolder commander. the man who dreamed up the whole enterprise, for instance, Churchill himself, or the impetuous Patton, called in many times during the stalemate – where could Operation Shingle have got to? Seeing that the enemy was not to be found, would Churchill and Patton have had the courage to jog on towards Rome with only two divisions, which could hardly have avoided exposing their flank and their back to the inevitable German counter-attack?

That is the real point. The supremacy in the air, which was evident in the efforts undertaken to prevent the Panzers and the cannons of Kesserling from concentrating in the area of the landing, would not have been enough to ensure the protection of the troops on the march, and far away from their bases. The great opportunity was lost, too, because the Liberty, the landing ship tanks (LST's) and the landing ship infantry (LSI's), those great container so painstakingly gathered together by Churchill would have had to perform a 'tour de force': return to Naples, pick up another two divisions (the 1st Armored led by General E.R. Harmon, and the 45th Infantry of General Eagles) and transport them to Anzio-Nettuno. The coming and going concluded at the end of January, when by now Colonel-General von Mackensen, Lucas opposite number. Had the same force available to him and was awaiting a further four divisions to move on to the counter-attack. Lucas tried to come out of his shell on 30th January, bet he was checked both at Cisterna and Campoleone. On the right, the massacre of two Ranger battalions; on the left, The English could barely get from Aprilia to the Campoleone station.

ANZIO-NETTUNO BEACH HEAD

The period from 22nd to 28th January, in short, can be seen as the fleeting moment which the Allies were unable to seize, when the ball was sitting there in front of the Germans' open goal. Ws it possible that despite the constant air reconnaissance and the network of collaborators who listened in to the enemy and never let them out of their sight, Alexander and the general staff were unaware of the breach in the German ranks south of Rome? As we have seen, in the case of Canaris regarding the imminent invasion. It was not only Kesserling who was badly hit by spying blunders, intentional or otherwise.

One of the most controversial decision in the was in Italy, that of the bombardment which destroyed the Abbey of Montecassino on 15th February, was probably provoked by a mistaken translation into English of one word in the exchange of brief phrases between one post of the Wehrmacht and another, which were intercepted by radio. Not very much for a mortal decision. The Abbot Gregorio Diamare, 82 years old, who emerged from the ruins holding a great wooden crucifix at eh head of about ten survivors, would never forgive the Allies, especially the English and Bernard Freyberg, the impulsive commander of the New Zealanders. But if Alexander, who was sorely pressed at that moment, needed a push to persuade him to order the bombardment, it was possibly that same interception, presented as proof of the Germans' presence in the monastery, that provided it for him.

At Nettuno-Anzio, on the other hand where Lucas was living at No. 16A Piazza del Mercato (Market Square), and had his command headquarters at No. 9, now No. 13 Via Romana (the entrance of the former 'Osteria dell'Artigliere – Wine seller of the artilleryman', the intercepted messages had never erred by as much as a comma. The English, the inventor of the instrument known as 'Ultra' which decoded German messages, in fact congratulated themselves on it. Another accusation has been leveled at Lucas as a result: "Since Kesserling's messages appealing for reinforcements from the north and from outside Italy had been translated for him immediately after the landing, why then was he still not lifting a finger?".

Because it was already too late: it should have been known about ten days earlier. But Ultra was in the front line; certainly it was not to be expected that Mrs Tortora, who had infiltrated the officers' high command in Piazza Mazzini, would provide an exact description of Kesserling's situation. Nor would the services of the secret agents, most of them Italian-Americans, who had been put ashore by submarines in rubber dinghies during the night, be enough (about thirty of the detachment of the US Office of Strategic Service 'OSS' who went ashore directly below the Sangallo Fortress which became their headquarters. (These were not the same men who had come, a few days and even a few hours before the actual landing to take soundings of the water depth and the characteristics of the coastline, and to provide a reference point for the amphibian craft). The people of Anzio and Nettuno were at first unaware of the presence of the secret agents who mingled with them, certainly there were new faces, but they possessed convincing identity cards: refugees coming from the countryside around the Garigliano River, where the war was raging. These refugees disappeared when the Allies arrived, and later the people of Nettuno and Anzio found them standing before them with a very different kind of authority: that of the uniform of the US Army.

Churchill himself, we must say, was unaware of the degree to which Kesserling had been forced to cut back his defenses in January to meet the attack of the Fifth Army along the Gustav Line. Had he known this, he would not have made such an effort to persuade Roosevelt of the need for the landing, and the army placed under Lucas' command would have been of quite different caliber. This can also be gathered from his memoirs. Deprived of direct information, he had to trust to the enemy, relying on the account of General Westphal: "At the moment of the landing south of Rome, apart from certain coastal batteries standing by, there were only two battalions... There was nothing else in the neighborhood which could be thrown against the enemy on that same day. The road to Rome was open. No one could have stopped a bold advance-guard entering the Holy City. The desperate situation continued for the first two days after the landing. It was only then that German counter-measures were effectives". (Westphal, *Op. cit.*, p. 242).

This confirm what we were saying earlier. However, Churchill makes no bones about quoting it in order to lend weight to his own cause. Was he or was he not right (we seem to hear him asking) to insist on the landing? And wasn't it more than justified to take up swords with Lucas, who had wrecked his whole scheme with his timorous approach? A feather in the cap for Churchill's intuition, we repeat for having put his finger on the weak point of the enemy line-up. But in fact, he had only just laid a finger on it, and had no right to demand from Lucas what had not been agreed with him.

The Prime Minister's conscience was not totally clear in this matter. He must have remembered the bitter conclusion that he had come to after the shilly-shallying with Eisenhower and the agreement with Roosevelt. He was immediately overjoyed by the latter, as we know. When he reflected on it, he could not avoid adding: "But I must also admit that I was so much occupied in fighting for the principle that I did not succeed in getting, and indeed did not dare to demand, the necessary weight and volume for the "cat-claw". Actually there were enough L.S.T.'s for the operation as planned... and we could, without prejudice to any other pledge or commitment, have flung ashore south of the Tiber a still larger force with full mobility... If I had asked for a three-division lift I should not have got anything. How often in life must one be content with what one can get! Still it would be better to do it right". (Churchill, *Op. cit.* p. 385).

To have got it right? How? Churchill might also have borne in mind what Alexander wrote eighteen day before the landing: "My experience of combined operations is that the initial assault to get ashore can be effected, but the success of the operation depends on whether the full fighting strength of the expedition can be concentrated in time to withstand the inevitable counter-attack. For Anzio, two division are the minimum force to

put ashore in face of likely resistance. (Churchill, Op.cit. p. 395).
There was in fact no resistance, but Lucas did not means to take advantage of the fact. There no getting away from this. Churchill was given a lesson on this score by Montgomery, who had been called by him to Marrakech where he was convalescing after pneumonia. Montgomery had already been chosen for the Normandy landing and, after handed over the command of the Eighth Army to General Oliver Leese, was flying back to Britain from Italy. In his villa in Marrakech, the Prime Minister could not wait to show him the plans for Operation Overlord, the fruit of months of study. The brains of the general staff, permanently stationed in London, had sweated blood over it. But Montgomery was one of those who cannot begin their working day without their morning run. He glanced through the first page and said immediately: "This will not do, I must have more in the initial punch".
In London, they were by no means in agreement, and the discussion dragged on. In the end, the eggheads had to give way and change their plan. When it came to the proof the modification demanded by Montgomery, as Churchill hastened to recognize, "was proved to be perfectly justified". Unfortunately for Anzio-Nettuno there was no-

one like Montgomery available at the time of decision. He would have dug his heels in and refused to move with two divisions. It was only this that Lucas actually erred. Instead of leaving on an expedition in which he did not believe, he should have offered his resignation, as Admiral Cunningham, from whom he had not hidden his lack of confidence, suggested he should.

A MOTORBIKE AND THE JEEPS

If we want to illustrate the surprise factor that characterized the landing of 22nd January 1944 without being too long-winded here are two cases. (One can't be 100 percent sure about the first, even though historians have often used it in their books.) The first example is German: it has to do with a motorbike and sidecar, perhaps a BMW with protruding cylinders, or else a DKW. It was on this motorbike, no later than two thirty a.m. as soon as he discovered that it was not just a matter of the usual disturbances, that a corporal of the engineers leapt and raced like a hell-hound along the Nettunense Highway.

For those who find it hard to believe this, there is also the word of honor of an officer, Lieutenant Heuritsch, posted to e regiment stationed at Sezze. He has recounted that, while he was travelling from Rome, his car was forced to stop on the road to Albano by the sharp braking of the corporal's motorbike. On learning his grave news Lieutenenat Heuritsch immediately found a way of commu-nicating with Kesserling and warning him. And if the telephone and the radio, and we might even add the television, weren't on the table in front of us, this might be taken as a tall story.

ANZIO-NETTUNO BEACH HEAD

But it seems, nevertheless, that reduced as they were to skeleton staff and sunk in sleep, the Nettuno Garrison had not even woken up to set off the alarm with an SOS, either by cable or over the air. History often feeds on legends, and that of the German motorcyclist, though the aims and the state of mind are very different, could be compared with th4 race from Marathon to Athens by the runner Philipides.

We turn now to second case. A history journalist, Arrigo Petacco, always ready for a scoop among the archives and war documents, was among the first to confirm an episode which was too readily set aside as idle chatter by the Nettuno-Anzio combatants. He used it to stress the inactivity of General Lucas and of the troops which had just landed. He wrote in a reminiscence in 1979: "The Allies, had they wanted to could have arrived in the capital in a few hours, as indeed one daring American journalist in a jeep actually did".

This was not fable, nor was it a bit of American showing off. The journalist didn't act alone, just for the sake of playing the cowboy. The jeep of an officer of the 3rd Division with his driver, and two other jeeps in which eight or ten advance reconnaissance scouts had taken their place along with the war correspondent himself (in uniform and carrying arms) all took part in that raid. But did they actually reach Rome, or were they only able to admire it from afar, for instance from the heights of Cecchina (where the climb begins to Albano), or from the fork at Frattocchie? Perhaps the imagination has taken a bit of a hold of those who claim that the patrol actually drove along the Appian highway to the point of passing unobserved, right in front of the sentries at the aerodrome at Ciampino which was then on full alert. What is undoubtedly true, in any case, is that whether or not his observation post was near or far, he did see the sun rise (and indeed it had already risen, but was not yet free and gay) over the fatal hills, the first houses and the ruins of the ancient Roman aqueducts.

An eye-witness account comes from Port Chester, a small town 25 miles from New York. It was there that the soldier who has made himself Nettuno's friend more than any other, Sgt. John Vita or Giovanni to his friends in Nettuno, was born and was still living. He was in his seventies then, but still very active and spent much of his time painting. He was a son of Italian emigrants. His father, Giuseppe, from Calabria who came originally from Scilla, emigrated to the USA in 1905, followed by his wife Rosaria two years later. Giovanni had already got a long way with his talents before he joined up: 20th Century Fox had taken him on as a cartoon designer. He was no Walt Disney admittedly, but there wasn't much he didn't know about films, and this enabled him to join the Fifth Army with his film camera and became one of General Clark's favorites. The latter took a great deal of care about his image, and not just in front of the mirror. (Such a rebuke was also heard in London and Washington against the otherwise greatly esteemed generals Montgomery and Patton, who were equally sensitive to photo coverage and newspaper headlines.)

Giovanni had his moment of glory on the occasion of the liberation of Rome. He was the first of the Americans to throw open the great door of the Venice Palace, and race up the staircase, for a scene which he must have dreamt up in Hollywood. Anyone who has seen Charlie Chaplin's parody of Hitler, or Jack Oakie in the role of Mussolini, will be able to picture Giovanni at that moment. The correspondent of 'Life' magazine began his report from Rome, published on 19th June 1944, with these words: "U.S. Sherman tanks entered the city decked with flowers. Jeeps rode past St. Peter's, while Piper Cubs flew overhead. Sgt. John Vita, of Port Chester, N.Y., made a speech from Old Mushmouth's balcony at the Piazza Venezia, as he had promised his mother he would do", he wanted to make clear, however, that the speech did not end with the shout: "...and for the Allies, eja, eja, alalà!".

How did it conclude? "Let's say", Giovanni answered, "as it began. It was 7 in the morning of the 5th June. Before opening the window of the balcony I had to stop. The height, the length and breadth of that green marble room! It was astonishing. Mussolini's desk was tall and huge as well. When I leaned out over the balcony, there were only a few people there; I started throwing 'Lifesaver' candies down to them. The people started gathering, and little by little the square filled up. As they were all there with their noises in the air, expecting something from me, I started to speak. Just a few words, however: I said: "Victory! Victory! Not for Mussolini but for the Allies". And I concluded: "We won't give you castor oil, but 'caramelli' and food!".

At Anzio-Nettuno, on the other hand, he gave no sign of being a public orator when he disembarked with General Truscott. It's easy to understand that as he hung around listening to the words of his commander, he felt it was his duty to be silent. We welcomed him to Nettuno many years ago; he told us he had returned to take a glass of wine with his old friends. At the Villa Donati, where for four months he had not merely exchanged places with the Germans but had become part of the family, they didn't find him changed at all. There was still that same reserve as when people used to ask him why the was never seemed to finish and he would just listen as though it had nothing to do with him; and if he were questioned he would just shrug his shoulder and change the subject. Only one evening, irritated by someone who accused the Americans of having landed with their eyes blindfolded, did he let himself go, and all of a sudden talked about the patrol which got to the gates of Rome.

Why not call him and ask for a confirmation? At his Port Chester number: 001/914/9393542 we've often caught him with a mouthful, because of the time-lag.

-Excuse us calling at this hour Giovanni.
"No problem. Sorry I can't let you taste my pasta and beans!".
-Thanks. But is the story of the jeep that went to Rome on the morning of the landing really true?
"Sure".
-Are you certain? Who did you hear it from?
"Not from anyone. I was there, when the officer told us that the road was clear...".
-And what about you? How did the command reply?
"We had to come back at once".

ANZIO-NETTUNO BEACH HEAD

-Then?
"Them the patrol went back to Nettuno. It wasn't yet eleven in the morning. There were a lot of soldiers gathered around the officer-in-charge. I think they wanted to make sure he talked directly with Truscott".
-Why was no move made after that?
"We were not supposed to move. Clark had made that very clear. Our job was to keep the Germans occupied".
Clark himself, for his part, was there at his post on the 22nd January. At three o'clock in the morning he had received from the 'Biscayne' Lucas' first message: "Paris- Bordeaux- Turin- Tangeries- Bari- Albania". According to the code-book this meant: "Sky clear, sea calm, wind little, our presence not discovered, landing in progress, reports from land imminent". Two hours later, with Alexander, he boarded a torpedo-boat in the mouth of the Volturno River to get to Nettuno-Anzio. It is unthinkable that these two, impatient, excited by the news, did not ask themselves, as they approached at great speed: "What do we do next?".
And this is what they did, according to the version given by Vaughan-Thomas, who followed Alexander closely. He saw him in a jeep passing along the sea front between Anzio and Lavinio:

elegant in a leather jacket with a sheep skin collar, with boots and gloves and a peaked cap. He was accompanied by Admiral Troubridge, who had come off the 'Bulolo'. Alexander stopped to have a few words with the soldiers and officers, giving his approval: "All right". With the same words, before re-embarking for Naples, he and Clark greeted Lucas: "All right".

Therefore the obvious conclusion of Vaughan-Thomas: "Whatever their reason for not applying the spur to Lucas, General Alexander and General Clark sailed from the Beachhead in the afternoon leaving the impression behind them that they were satisfied with the progress made and that they approved the policy of waiting for the German counter-attack...They came, they saw, they concurred". (Vaughan-Thomas, *Op. cit.* p. 51).

This would be enough to exonerate Lucas before any court. The one who doesn't come out well from the affair is Alexander. In justification it has been claimed that his dispositions were not respected, and that Clark himself changed the cards on the table. In effect, his order which assigned the expedition the task of "cutting the enemy's communications in the region of the Alban Hills, to the south-east of Rome, and menacing the gathering-point of the 14th German Army" had been modified by Clark and passed on to Lucas on

12th January in the following form: "1) constitute a beachhead near Anzio; 2) consolidate its possession; 3) advance towards the Alban Hills". Not content with this, Clark explained more clearly to his subordinate, in a confidential recommendation: "Don't stick your neck out. I did it at Salerno and got into trouble".

It seems like a droll story from the days of the Bourbon Army. If he was unable to make his wishes respected what kind of commander was Alexander? There is no need, however, to be too harsh with him. Not even the exalted discipline of the Wehrmacht saved Kesserling from similarly violating ("unfortunately changing" was the expression used) his orders or from failing to carry them out, both at Cassino and on the Anzio-Nettuno front.

Easier said than done. The same thing happens to newspaper editors who have all the autonomy proper to their job on paper, but in practice have to bow to the wishes of the proprietors, who in defiance of statutes and labor contracts, can sack them or replace them at will, even for supporting a different political trend. We submit, let it be clear, that Churchill's greatness is all the more outstanding. His superior character and his diplomacy, united with Roosevelt's loyalty (for this part Roosevelt look little interest in military matters and relied heavily on General Marshall) never failed, even if, as in our case, some compromise had to be made. But when it came to confronting the pig-headedness of De Gaulle, who was downright contemptuous of Roosevelt, Churchill put him in his place with one of those warnings which leave no room for doubt: "Did he not realize how much difficulty he made for himself in the United States? How angry the President was with him? How much was all depended on American aid goodwill?". (Churchill, *Op. cit.*,p.401).

Alexander could hardly fail to feel the effects of this situation because Clark and the Fifth Army were under his command. Conditioning was inevitable. In any case, it was no part of a great general's way of behavior to play the game of 'pass the buck' with someone who, together with Clark, had in practice signed the condemnation of his subordinate Lucas. Why was there not even a word of solidarity from Churchill? Whatever his natural caution with the Americans, he let his real feeling be known to the representatives of those governments close to him.

The disappointment and the polemics which it led to in Great Britain made it necessary for him to come to the House of Commons on 22nd February and explain the facts and answer questions. On the next day, the most enlightened of the Commonwealth leaders, The magnificent Jan Christian Smuts (the man who had done everything possible for the reconciliation of the English and the Boers and against the arguments of the neutralists, had warned to bring South Africa into the struggle against Nazism) telegraphed him to congratulate him on this intervention. However, he didn't refrain from criticism: "I myself have not followed our strategy in the Anzio beach-head, which I had thought would link up with the Cassino front with the object of breaking German resistance in the southern mountains. An isolated pocket has now been created which is unconnected with the enemy's main front...". (Churchill, Op.cit. p. 435).

From the military standpoint, the old General's observations seems to centre the target. With the resources of the 6th Corps, perhaps the error was to have aimed at the Alban Hills, instead of aiming behind the Gustav Line. But leaving aside personal responsibility, was the Prime Minister really wrong in lamenting the fact that no advantage was taken from the uncontested landing in order to take the Alban Hills? The subsequent disposition of the German troops (it was only necessary to give the password 'Case Richard', which was the alarm-bell for the eventuality of a landing south of Rome, to bring the divisions racing down from the north of Italy, and also from France, from Yugoslavia and from Germany) made it clear that the fate of Lucas's men would have been sealed if they had left the sea shore.

Kesserling anyway, had no doubts on this point. His fear dissolved as soon as he was able to put binoculars to his eyes and from the slopes of Monte Cavo, along with General von Mackensen, observe the ant-like movements of the Anglo-Americans along the coast. It was not difficult for him to see that the numbers were not very great: "A half measure", he commented. Alexander must have agreed at least in part. Would it have been possible, the question was asked after the war, to have preserved the links with Anzio and repel the enemy counter-offensive in an area which would have included the Alban Hills? "It would", he replied, "have been an extremely difficult undertaking".

General Truscott on the other hand expressed himself without reserve, and with no regard at all for those who thought like Churchill. We must remember that this was the man who replaced Lucas on 23rd February in the box, according to one of the rules of football which says that if a team doesn't win, it's never the fault of the management but always of the coacher. And in addition to packing his bags, the latter often has to stand by and see his own No. 2 promoted over his head, and hear him declare to a press conference: "Now you'll see. I am going to change everything". Truscott didn't behave like that at all.

Like Churchill, Alexander, Clark, Kesserling and Westphal, he did not fail to collect material during the war to produce yet another book 'Command Missions'. For the sake of peace, to avoid reproducing war, it might be better if the main actors did not say anything more about their enterprises, because these become teaching matter later for the military academies. That is another story, however. In any case, Truscott sang out loud and clear: "All the armchair strategists never stop arguing in the mistaken belief that there was a lost opportunity at Anzio of which some modern Napoleon might have been able to profit in order to throw himself at the Alban Hills, put a spoke in the wheel of German communications, and gallop as far as Rome. Such ideas reveal a complete incomprehension of the military problem which faced us. We had to constitute a solid defense ahead of the beach-head, in order to prevent the enemy from attacking the beaches. If we had ignored this concern, the German artillery and the armored detachments operating on our flanks would have been able to cut us off from the coast, preventing the landing of troop, supplies and material". (Lucian K. Truscott, *Command Missions*, p. 311).

'The missed opportunity' did however exist, and we have Churchill's own word for it. The picture of what really happened has been ably Samuel Eliot Morison, official historian of the US Navy. In the ninth volume of his patient reconstruction of all the naval operations of the Second World War, his synthesis makes short work of all the doubts about this issue. "It was the only amphibian operation in which the army was incapable of taking rapid advantage of a landing which had been perfectly successful, and in which the enemy succeeded in containing the Allied forces for a long period in the beach-head. In the whole war, there is nothing which can be compared with Anzio. Even the Okinawa campaign in the Pacific was shorter.

The army's incapacity, we must now conclude, was not the incapacity of Lucas, but the consequence of the compromise which Churchill had had to agree to. He believed in the landing. The Americans now deeply concerned with the possibility of dealing direct blow at the heart of Germany through Normandy, were less convinced about it, and ended up by backing the Prime Minister against their will and not giving him everything he needed (we need only mention that for Overlord 3605 landing-craft were put at Eisenhower's disposal in order to land 12 divisions, while Operation Shingle had few more than 230 to transport, in relays, 4 divisions).

What then, urged Churchill on? Only the initiative of a gambler? The respect which is due to him and the tragic balance – the death of thousands of men, the armies curtailed in the mud of the tranches, the villages razed to the ground, the refugees now no longer five kilometers but hundreds of kilometers away from the things they held dearest – make it inadmissible to make conjectures and hasty judgments. But we cannot get away from the problem, at least from our observation point, of the tentacles of mystery N.1 of all wars; that of the spying which always seems to lurk behind great events. Its part in the affair of Anzio-Nettuno has also been recounted by General William J. Donovan, an American less well-known and quoted than Alexander, Clark, Lucas and Truscott, and yet present in everything they did, as head of the Office of Strategic Service (OSS), the military information service later replaced by the CIA.

According to his calculations, which perhaps were based too much on the psychological effect of the landing and the conviction that the enemy's morale was at its lowest, the Germans – with a threat at their backs - would not have been able to avoid abandoning their positions at Cassino, and withdrawing in haste, as had happened in Sicily. In order to achieve this, two divisions would have been enough. But the calculations of Donovan and his spies were mistaken.

However, Churchill, replaying to Smuts' telegram on 27th February, did not limit himself to criticizing the Americans. Nor did he stop at sharpening the medicine for Lucas, the fifty-four-years old general "dominated by the idea that at all costs he must be prepared for a counter-attack". Nor did he refrain from attacking Clark, who had sent the 504th P.I.R. by sea, and treated them as if they were normal infantry. Neither did he stop repeating that he had in vain "sent Alexander instructions that he should peg out claims rather than consolidate beach-heads". The indomitable Prime Minister concludes in his best manner: "I do not in any way repent of what has been done. As a result, the Germans have now transferred I into the south of Italy at least eight more divisions, so that in all there are eighteen south of Rome. It is vital to the success of Overlord...". (Churchill, *Op. cit.*, p.436).

As, in fact, was to be shown.

The Allies' arrival was immediately welcomed as the end of the war. Even in Rome, which was hardly just around the corner, it was difficult to hold back the exultation, with the thundering of the guns and the flashes which could be seen from the direction of the sea, everyone was convinced that liberation was already under way. It was a question of hours, and the jeeps would be arriving from the Appia highway the chase the tortures out of Via Tasso. The first to have no doubts about this were three fathers of our new democracy, Ivanoe Bonomi, Alcide De Gasperi and Pietro Nenni, who had all taken refuge in the Seminary of St. John Lateran. Bonomi acted ax the leader of the Committee of National Liberation for Central Italy. He had been awakened at dawn by a code message which announced in advance the end of the German oppression: "Your aunt is ill and about to die".

The confirmation came a few hours later from the group of refugees in the Vatican. The secretary of Baron Ernst von Weizsaecker, the German Ambassador to the Holy See, had revealed to one of their friends that Colonel Dollman and the Chief of the Gestapo, Herbert Kappler, were packing their bags: "We think that in two or three days, they will be withdrawing from the capital". They must, therefore have been given marching orders. Giorgio Amendola, the Commander of the GAP (Patriotic Action Groups) was already raising the banner for acts of sabotage while 'L'Unità', in its secret printing press, was preparing a special edition with the nine-column headline "Rose rises up".

One of the most daring secret agents came out into the open: the American Peter Tompkins. He belonged to OSS and on that very morning of the 22nd January, having set out from Corsica with an Italian MTB and landed in a rubber canoe somewhere south of Orbetello, had reappeared in the centre of Rome. He knew the city like the back of his hand, having worked there as a correspondent of the New York 'Herald Tribune' before the war. Completely convinced that he could finish off the Germans and provoke an uprising among the Romans, Tompkins vainly sent General Clark a plan for the immediate launching of the parachute regiment right in the middle of Piazza di Siena, the riding track only a step away from the Porta Pinciana.

He didn't take long for a cold shower to douse all this euphoria. Five days after the landing, at the London address of 'Colonel Wardden' (Churchill's code name), a dispatch from Alexander began the series of bad news with the words: "We aere still on the coast, Campoleone and Cisterna have not been taken". The general made it clear to the prime Minister that it was no longer possible to be satisfied with Lucas. However, up to that point, the liberation had been a reality for the people of Anzio and Nettuno. They had it there, before their eyes, in the sea full of ships and in the last Germans' final episode: two of them on foot and one on a bicycle, were seen searching for an escape route through the tracks at Cioccati area, after having thrown their uniforms behind a bush. For the six Nettuno women imprisoned in the stables of the command in Piazza Mazzini, in the dark, amidst the filth, their hands tied to the rings formerly used for tethering the horses, it was indeed liberation.

ANZIO-NETTUNO BEACH HEAD

A British sniper amongst the ruins of Aprilia, watch out for German soldiers. The little town of Aprilia, built in 1936 and inaugurated in 1937, was on hands of the British troops until middle February. It passed to the German side after Operation Fishfang (16-19 February, 1944), until 28th of May 1944.

THE FORTUNE-TELLER

Their names were Chiara, Mimma, Rosetta, Pina, Adelaide and Natalina. They were saved by e real miracle. They were all mothers, family women advanced in years. They all died except Natalina.

We went to see her, and we discovered a quite eccentric personality, probably formed in that dreadful prison where along with her friends she spent four days condemned to death. This person, whose name in the Registry Office is Natalina Grattoni, born in 1904, is better known as the Fortune-teller Lina, or Lina the Fortune-teller. She had always possessed the gift of looking into the future. Even as a young amateur while she was still cashier at the Grand'Italia in Via Romana (later the Capitol Cinema), she never missed a chance to show off her talents. At 84, she must have been a great expert, to judge from the clientele, for the most part women, who queue up each day outside the door.

She lived alone, in one of the first houses in Via Lombardia, though she did make use of the service of a companion in the hours when she was seeing her clients (from four to six in the afternoons). We must say that as we saw her for a minute or two, half deal and half blind, through the half-open door, she gave us the impression of having retired with the ghosts, absorbed in something which no-one else could fell or see. However, if she is capable of seeing into the future, she shows no desire to remember the past. She sent us away very rapidly: "Yes, yes, it was the Americans who freed me. Why do you want to talk about it again?"

The story of Chiara, Mimma, Rosetta, Pina, Adelaide and Natalina, then, began on 17th January when the food supply in the Campana area was finished. It seemed to be worth their while to risk even the execution order, rather than face death by starvation. They took the train to Rome, and managed to pick up something on the black market in piazza Vittorio. On their return they were blocked by an air-raid at the station at Campoleone and forced to make a dash for it. But they just couldn't get through; the German SS picked them up at Campo di Carne.

The sentence was "Kaputt" – execution. In the prison they found other women and boys already chained up. The Germans were waiting for the evening, when they would select them three at a time (two boys and a woman, two women and a boy, and so on). Afetr that, nothing more remained of each trio but the rumble of gunshot at the wall of death.

"On the last evening", Natalina said, "about twelve of us were left, and we were all in great dread about whom they were going to choose. But they didn't come. After a bit we dozed off, but then we were awaken by the incessant noise of a heavy bombardment. It lasted until the morning. I had already gone four days without relieving myself, because of the shame; suddenly they came at dawn and released us all; untied us and let us out. We told each other: 'It's the end', and I added to myself that it was better that way, but these soldiers seemed to use much nicer methods than the other lot".

So much 'nicer', in fact, that they provided the unfortunates not only with freedom, but with a complete service. They were taken up to the upper floor of what really deserved the name of "Palazzaccio (Bad Building)", more than the Palace of Justice in Rome, and there they were washed, dried and disinfested; they were given clothes, wool sweaters, underwear, shirts, stockings, a pair of clogs each, and finally all sat down around a table and had soup and tins of meat and beans, cheese, chocolate powdered milk and coffee. "From the window we could see a cloud of balloons and the sea jammed with ships. It was the American landing: it was only then that we realized how lucky we'd been". Thus the fortune-teller who no longer wanted to remember finished her story.

In archives of the memory, these things tend to cloud-over. But in Nettuno and Anzio one image has remained intact of that morning when they finally realized what had happened; it has stayed clear amid the dust of nearly seventy-five years. This is the picture of the sea so full of ships that it could no longer be seen. If it had been due to the phenomenon of an interminable low tide, which had drawn the sea back all along the shore for several miles, then at least the sea-bed would have been visible. But it seemed rather that the earth had moved forward and filled it up entirely, from Torre Astura to Anzio, and this was in fact the effect created: a black mountain of ships, side by side, lined up one behind the other just like those cars parked these days in all our big cities, forming a sort of metal covering to all the major squares.

The spectacle has remained with those who witnessed it. "At 5, 5:30 am and still at 6 am, remembered Fernanda, the niece of Pietro and Ciro Donati, we were all on the terrace. More than the explosions and cannonades during the night, what struck us was the hasty departure of the Germans; they had suddenly abandoned the villa. We came upstairs from the cellar, first cautiously and then running. Our terrace was the highest in the town then. From up there, on a clear day, you could see across to Ponza island. But that morning, there was no more see. What struck me above all was the balloons hanging like bunches of grapes over the ships. They explained that they were there to protect them from low-flying air attacks, but they looked for all the world as they were holding them fast, more effective then anchors".

To contribute to keeping the Donati brothers awake that night there had been another unexpected event. On the previous day at Otricoli, in the province of Terni, theur parental grandmother, Adele, had died; and because they didn't know how they could manage the voyage from Nettuno, a car had left Umbria to collect the Donatis and take them to the funeral. The car was not precisely a taxi, but that was its function, especially in those villages where there were few people with driving licenses. When it was necessary to hire a car, a driver had to be found as well. In the case of the Donatis, the owner of the hire-car himself Bramante Pagliari, took the wheel. He was a fine imposing man, and his car, a Lancia Augusta, third series, four doors, its number-plate TR 3971 had everything to ensure that it would be noticed. Among other things, it had belonged to the Nettuno station-master, who had sold it a year earlier through a motor salesroom in Rome.

An odd coincidence, on which it would be hard not to remark. Indeed, it seems to confirm that Bramante's journey was destined to be one without a return; he, it must be said, was the first victim the people of Nettuno and Anzio had to record in the balance-sheet of the landing. From Otricoli he had brought with him his fifteen-year-old son Mario, and he had had a great trouble, after reaching Piazza Mazzini, in getting to the villa. Certainly the address was written down on a piece of paper. But at nine in the evening, with the Germans not leaving a single lamp alight and all the houses empty, with never a soul in sight, whose door could be knock on to find the way? The more they drove around father and son, the more they found themselves back where they had started. It was one of the Margherita Ricci bakers who finally solved their problem, as eleven o'clock struck: they were a few yards from their destination.

It was not the moment for the Donatis to indulge in formalities. However, Ciro and Pietro were unable to move from there, and the arrangements was that only Ada should go to the funeral. At dawn, naturally, it was enough to take a look at the balloons and ships to realize that any project of the kind would come to nothing. Bramante didn't waste any time on the terrace. He turned to his son and said: "Let's hurry or we'll be trapped here". The Donatis, unfortunately their words went unheeded, tried to dissuade him, and in any case refused to allow Ada to leave. Instead, Giuseppe Moroni, another Nettuno man who needed a lift so that he could join his family which had evacuated to Rome, left with Bramante and his son.

Half an hour later, as he drove along Via Gramsci, in his Lancia Augusta, the hire-car owner from Otricoli was killed by accident. He had had to stop and drive near the wall of the Villa Borghese, because the road was covered in glass, strange fragments smeared with a gelatinous substance. "Go and clear them out of the way, otherwise we'll get the tire perforated", he said to his son. Mario had only taken a few steps when he was stopped short by Moroni's cry: "Stop! Stop! Put your hands up, quick". He turned round; he saw Moroni himself outside the car with his hands above his head. He saw the car door on his father's side open. Then there was a rattle of machine-guns, and he saw no more.

At the point at which Bramante fell, a little before the small building surrounded by a wall which was later let to residents, there is plaque hearing this inscription: "During the attempt to rejoin his family he was shot down for no reason". Don Steno had it put up at the end of the war. But Mario was arrested immediately afterwards with Moroni, and taken like a prisoner of war to the cellars of the unauthorized gambling house which till today is the uninhabited 'Paradiso'. Here he met Prince Borghese who was also imprisoned. He was not yet aware of his father's death. He talked to the Prince about what had happened, and the latter, who was beginning to clear himself with the Americans, was authorized to accompany him to look for his father. The remains of the Lancia Augusta, completely destroyed looked as if it had a direct hit from a hand grenade. Don Steno, who was ahead, saw the body of Bramante first, lying on the pavement, with the jacked thrown aside. He stopped Mario from coming nearer and led him away.

What was the cause of the error? It was one of the Rangers who fired the shot. Certainly the appearance of that Lancia Augusta, driving rapidly out of a place where the enemy was believed to be hiding, had been mistaken at that hour of the day for an escape attempt by the fascists or Germans in civilian disguise. It could also be that Bramante who, being a big man, always took a long time getting out of his car, had made a movement without realizing it that seemed like a threat: for instance, a hand in his jacket as if to get out a weapon. Presumably there was something that is if there is any logic in human illogic.

Mario was released after a few days. Looked after by the Donati family until the liberation of Rome, he made every effort in those four months to get to know more, asking questions of every American soldier he met. He wasn't even allowed to have the body of his father to take back to Otricoli; they told him that it could no longer be found. He got it into his head that he would find a machine-gun and kill at least three Rangers. It was John Vita, whom he had met at the Donatis and which whom he had become friends, who calmed him down: "It's the war which is to blame; it isn't our fault; it isn't anyone's fault".

The blame, however, lies with those who unleash was. Perhaps in the surprise factor, which disorientated both the Germans and the Allies, there is also to be found the origin of the absurd death of the car-hire man from Otricoli.

Alexander and Clark, apart from arming their expedition, had also had to concern themselves with other seemingly secondary problems, such as the first contact and relations with the inhabitants of Anzio-Nettuno. It was above all a matter of re-erecting as an administrative necessity, an edifice that had collapsed.

The solution, in peace and for peace, could not ne other than the one guaranteed by Roosevelt and Churchill: democracy. In other words, self-determination for the Italian people. Although the Allies were agreed on this in principle, they were less so in the course of the political events that induced even the military leadership to pronounce themselves against Victor Emmanuel III.

For General Headquarters in Algiers, where he had taken over Eisenhower's post, Henry Maitland Wilson, known as 'Jumbo', sent telegrams to the Chief of Staff in London and Washington, advocating the party of Italy which had been liberated, a government which would correspond to popular aspirations, and hence one based on the anti-fascist parties.

The telegram found a ready hearing in Washington. Roosevelt was of the same opinion. He wrote to Churchill: "In the present situation the Chief in Charge and the political advisers, both British and American, have recommended that we give immediate support to the program of the six Opposition parties. Thus we have, happily, for one, our political and military considerations entirely in harmony... I cannot for the life of me understand why we should hesitate any longer in supporting a policy so admirably suited to our common military and political aims. American

public opinion would never understand our continued tolerance and apparent support of Victor Emmanuel". (Churchill, *Op. cit.* p. 445-446).
However, Churchill thoughts otherwise. His defense of Victor Emmanuel III had been taken by historians to be the apologia of a conservative who, while devoting himself to the defeat of Nazi-fascism, had feared the spread of communism, or the "Boleshevisation", as he liked to call it, of the whole of Europe. He sought to use monarchies as a dyke to stern the flood, even though he had been among the first to support the popular uprisings, and had been so keen to help the partisans that he had even allowed his son Randolph to parachute into the ranks of Tito's supporters. And yet despite this he had fought to keep the throne for Peter II of Yugoslavia, and for King George II of Greece. However, it was only just that the English, should feel an obligation towards them, as Allies, that they could not feel towards Victor Emmanuel.
It was simply anti-communism which made Churchill so solicitous for the fate of the unfortunate monarchs. He had already been forced to justify this with Roosevelt, who in fact suspected some particular intrigue. "Victor Emmanuel is nothing to us, except for the fact that it was he, along with Badoglio, who put the Italian

fleet into our hands". General Wilson's stand confused him, but above all, it was a move by Stalin, who without consulting the Allies, had accredited a Russian ambassador to Badoglio's government, which made him stick to his guns: "I do not think it would be wise, without further consideration, to accept the program of the so-called Six Parties and demand forthwith the abdication of the King and installation of Signor Croce as Lieutenant of the Realm. I will however consul the War Cabinet upon what you justly call "a major political decision". (Churchill, *Op. cit.* p. 446).

He must have been furious to go so far as to use expressions like 'the so-called Six Parties' and 'Signor Croce' (the unsullied philosopher who had never lowered himself to compromise with Fascism, and whose works deserved much better both from Churchill and from Harold Macmillan, the High Commissioner, who described him as a 'dwarf 75 years old professor', bearing a strong resemblance to 'a gnome', after having tried to ingratiate himself with Croce with the pretext: "I have come to you on behalf of the English publishers of your books"). Once his self-control had run out, Churchill was anything but subtle. His judgment on Count Sforza, whom Roosevelt would have immediately preferred to Badoglio, was anything but affectionate: 'A vain and foolish old man, good for nothing'. Macmillan added further unfavorable judgment, regarding him 'a theatrical chatterbox'. To the President of the USA, there was nothing left but a few words of homage to Victor Emmanuel: "I am told that the old gentleman only functions before lunch".

But what did the War Cabinet, summoned urgently to meet, decide? The account which Churchill drew up to Roosevelt can be summarized in the following points:

1) That at the very least, the Allies should wait for the conquest of Rome before getting rid of the King and Badoglio;

2) That if they were eliminated, the task of the Allied armies would be complicated;

3) That it was yet to be demonstrated that the Six Parties effectively represented democracy and the Italian nation;

4) That the Six Parties themselves would not have been able to do better than the King and Badoglio, who since the day of the Armistice had loyally collaborated with the Anglo-Americans;

5) That Great Britain was not in agreement with the telegram sent around by General Wilson;

6) Lastly that, after the step taken by the Russians at Brindisi, nothing must be allowed to emerge of the divergence between London and Washington.

To put this back into chronological order, it all took place two months after the landing at Anzio-Nettuno, in preparing which, the English had more than one reason for not leaving out the 'King of Brindisi'. He was very much under the thumb of the Allied Military Government (which by no means failed to take an active interest in the civil administration, intervening with food supplies and also with that avalanche of paper which came out with the issue of the Am-lire) and he never failed to obey; and urged on Badoglio, he had found the courage to communicate to Hitler, through the Spanish ambassador, that at 15:00 hours on 13th October 1943, Italy would enter the war against Germany.

The match against the Salò regime, where the Fascist had rebuilt their party, which was playing a rival game, was becoming rough. How could one fail to be concerned about re-establishing legal government in the areas to be freed? Alexander sent Badoglio a request for men and material, but kept him completely in the dark about Operation Shingle; thus an Italian contingent was in fact included in the 6th Corps. This representation has been recorded by Raleigh Trevelyan, one of the youngest officers, hardly twenty years old, who ended up with his platoon in the trenches between Tor San Lorenzo and Ardea in the first days of

March. In his book 'Rome '44', first published y Martin Secker and Warburg in 1981, he describes it as 'a contingent of a hundred and fifty soldiers, who were unarmed however, and employed as dock workers. These were followed in March by seventy or so mechanics and an equal numbers of drivers. The former, commanded by Lieutenant Giovanni De Paoli were mostly from Rome, but there was Giuseppe Falconi from Abruzzo. The latter, brought from Sardinia by Captain Cominotti and given the task of refurbishing the front line with ten-wheel lorries, were all northerners except for Second Lieutenant Franco Roviglioni from Rome.

But where were the civilians? The Rangers spread out in a fan from the Zanardelli Riviera towards the port and the Villa Borghese, while the parachutists of the 509th battalion, also Americans, got to the big Piazzale della Divina Provvidenza, the terrace of the Belvedere, the Villino Talenti, the low walls of the Sangallo gate. The paratroops where in the centre of Nettuno. Before moving in to Piazza Mazzini, they waited for a long time like sprinters on all fours at the blocks before the final of the hundred meters dash. They did not have to make any sprint. Around them, as the darkness of the night disappeared, he shells of the open and uninhabited houses emerged. The only human sound was the echo of the ships' loudspeakers. These were guiding towards the shore the other detachments who, coming up from St. Rocco and 'Siren's Beach', completed the occupation of the town.

Slowly slowly the paratroops got on their feet and placing themselves to the right and left of the doorways, began to make themselves heard, since their specific task, was to occupy Nettuno and to flush out the enemy and to round up, or in the military terminology to 'mop up' every building. With their electric torches, and cracking their rifles against the grills of the ground-floor windows, they had already lured into Via Gramsci, outside one of the villas by the sea, four or five startled Germans who had expected anything but the Americans. The bodies of these Germans lay on the pavement about a hundred yards before the House of the Guardian Angels.

At first daylight "Officer began to recognize features from air photographs, an ancient watch-tower built once against the Saracens, silos and farm buildings – though all deserted. It was like landing in a ghost country, where ghosts could turn lethal". (Trevelyan, *Rome '44*, p. 43). Perhaps because of these sensations – to try to understand the absurd – it might happen that one doesn't stop to think about pulling the trigger on a harmless man who is taking a while to squeeze himself out of a Lancia Augusta.

Fear of the silence, the emptiness, and the void, to more than an error. But where were the people? The Rangers of Villa Borghese couldn't have known the answer at dawn on 22nd January. They learned later what we already knew; the history of Nettuno-Anzio under the Germans, with the deportations, the evacuation orders, the executions, the plundering and the people living in huts.

The only person the Rangers found at home was Don Steno, and ha was already up. He had seen them from his balcony and went down to meet them just as they were about to shoot his dog who had unwisely run out to bark at the strangers. He was in time to save him, but not to prevent machine-guns being pointed at the servants and himself as they were immediately lined up against the wall. They were all arrested and held for a day in the improvised prison, the white 'Paradiso'; as was the local policeman, Rodrigo Taurelli, who, as was his habit, had come to take his orders from Prince Borghese. As there didn't seem to be any other local people about, Trevelyan deduced that "there was very little for the 150 'Carabinieri' brought from Naples to do".

The 'Carabinieri' however soon had something to do. It is not exactly true that they were already in the ship on the night of the landing (and if we are to be really precise, there were 148 of them and not 150: 2 officers, 9 NCO's and 137 lance-corporals and other ranks). They arrived on 3rd February, almost two weeks later, and their journey was as bad as it could be, what with a stormy sea and the welcome by the Germans, who were by then keeping watch on the movements in the port of Anzio from the Roman Hills, and could target their guns on any boat approaching the jetty.

Right from the start things had been going badly for the contingent. They had been transported in eight lorries to the port of Naples, and had embarked the previous evening in one of those LST's which Churchill was so anxious to get hold of. They stayed there for hours, awaiting the signal to leave, which never seemed to come.

It was one of those days when it would be much better not to go near the sea: rain, wind and breakers which made the ferries run for shelter. With their clumsy landing-craft, they risked shipwreck. The counter-order arrived after midnight. The 'Carabinieri' back on shore, were loaded back into lorries and driven to Pozzuoli, from where at 4:30 in the morning they braved the storm in an American torpedo-boat.

It took them twelve hours to get from Pozzuoli to Nettuno-Anzio. There wasn't even space to turn around in the little vessel from the American fleet, and the spray and the waves poured over the deck. Crouched under cover, one on top of the other, they were all suffering from seasickness. The foul weather didn't even do them the favor of keeping the German air-force at bay, though by mere chance it missed its target. As also did the cannons greeting the 'Carabinieri' still offshore from Anzio. Amidst the bombs and the columns of water, the 148 'Carabinieri' disembarked, certain that this time they had arrived in hell.

The officer in charge of them was a Neapolitan layer Silvio Pezzella, who never imagined, with all the trouble the war had brought, that he would still be wearing his uniform as late as 1951, the year in which he finally left the service. He was the Captain in the Reserves, survivor of the Balkan front, confused like the majority of Italians at that stage, and devastated by the pile of ruins he had found in place of his home in Via Pietro Colletta, between the main road and the Porta Capuana. He had become a lieutenant colonel in retirement and lived between the sky and the sea on the heights of Posillipo, not far from the Fuorigrotta Stadium. He therefore enjoyed the virtuoso performances of Maradona (of whom he was a fan, as he was of

ANZIO-NETTUNO BEACH HEAD

Attila Sallustro in the other Naples Stadium, the Ascarelli). And he was comfortably satisfied with the promotions and honors he received from his military career.

He had joined the army as a 'Bersagliere', and moved to the 'Carabinieri' in 1940; he was attached to the Bolzano Legion, which put him in charge of holding the frontier at Vipiteno, before sending him off to Serbia. But the Military Cross for valour was awarded to him for his work in the area of Anzio-Nettuno. It was preceded by the citation for merit with which General Giuseppe Pieche, then Commander of the 'Carabinieri', honored him in the general exultation over the liberation of Rome: "Captain Silvio Pezzella, following the American Fifth Army, in the landing area heavily bombarded by the enemy, gave effective, intelligent and brave support to the Allied Command, earning their commendations".

His company placed at Lucas disposition with the label "Contingent R", was divided into three parts: the first – 25 men under the command of second lieutenant Francesco Farina – at Anzio; the second – 15 men under sergeant-major Giovanni Raimondo – at Nettuno, and the rest – under the Captain himself. It was close behind the front line. In the countryside which stretches from the Campana area towards the scrubland of the Armellino and the Padiglione woods. "In the wood", we learnt from Pezzella himself, "a number of General Harmon's tanks were hidden, and there were also cannons and a ammunitions dump belonging to the English. We were on the fringe, looking after surveillance. We slept in the trenches, with nothing more than our greatcoats, an army blanket and two canvas of the camouflage tent. All of this was our common stuff, even the weapons, which consisted of pistols and the usual '91 rifles. The Americans only gave us the motor vehicles for our reconnaissance for checking the isolated farmhouses (in which it was suspected that there might be some spies hiding, as well as deserters), and for escorting the refugees. These last gathered in the Church of St. Theresa, before being sent off to ships for their transfer to the south. My thoughts go to all the dead, but I especially regret the loss of my own 'Carabinieri', Pietro Chinchero and Mario Rossi, and the many unfortunate civilians who were unwilling to leave their land".

General Clark has been judged in many different ways. A native of Madison Barracks in New York, he never disguise the fact that he was a catholic; but with his height and his bony features he seemed to the English like an Apache Chief, a warrior and a medicine man at the same time, coming out of the west with his bow, his hatchet and his totem. On this last point everyone seems to agree, recognizing his continual concern for his personal image and public relations. In May 1944 when the Fifth Army passed the Garigliano it was thus to be expected that there would be an article over his signature in the Naples newspapers: in the city of the heroic dour days of resistance to the German forces, this was quite appropriate.

Clark's thanks to the Italians who had fought with him, however, did not mean that his failing could be simple ignored. Who, for instance, had equipped the 'Carabinieri' of Captain Pezzella? From Nettuno and Anzio to Cisterna, Aprilia, Tor San Lorenzo, there was no point at which at the very least the shrapnel was not flying – and there they were with their heads exposed to the four winds, or almost so. All they had was the classic three-cornered hat with its grey-green lining, except for Pezzella who wore a forage cap, pulled down a little over his right ear.

Lucas, who was one of those who never took his helmet off even at the table, was scandalized at this. Badoglio, Badoglio... Did he think they were taking part in a parade? It wouldn't have been illogical, either with his precedents and the initial success of the Allied landings, if the Brindisi Court had been setting itself up for another march on Rome in a carriage like that of Victor Emmanuel's cousin. Let us be realistic and put it down to carelessness and the element of degeneration which those responsible for fascism had introduced into Italy.

The Americans, who would have nothing to do with the King (as we know, they wanted to set him aside) made their voice heard also on this occasion. Badoglio could do nothing but climb down. We can image the shrill phone-calls which passed from the kingdom of Apulia to Naples, until finally a load of helmets of the Italian army left for Anzio. Now Pezzella and his men, with the undeniable advantage of covered heads, no longer had to face commiserations mockery. From the helmets 'made in Italy', in fact, they received an unexpected bonus, something which helped to raise their morale.

In Nettuno, every break was a chance for the Americans to bring out their kitbag their baseball bats and mitts: baseball was their favorite sport and it helped them to relax. The idea then came to them for another game, since they knew that the 'Carabinieri' helmets were different from theirs. The contest – for that's what it was – consisted in bashing one helmet against the other to see which was tougher. It was always the American ones which buckled. "At least there was one thing in which we were stronger, and didn't need to envy the Allies", the lieutenant colonel in retirement tells himself in consolation, even to those days!

The story of the 'Carabinieri' doesn't finish there: it would be incomplete if it didn't include that of the comrades in arms from Nettuno, who having taken off their uniform on 8th September 1943, put them on again during the German occupation, at least a month prior to the landing. There were eight of them: Sgt. Giuseppe Pitruzzello, from Melilli in the province of Syracusa, 2nd Sgt. Raffaele Di Iorio, and corporals Antonio Kammerlocher, Odero Bigotto, Gori, Marletta, Ovidi and another by the name of Peppino. The Germans raided their station – one of the building on Via St. Maria, beyond the Town Hall, but they had already made themselves scarce.

Except for Kammerlocher, who was married to Luigina Di Pietro from Nettuno, by this time a refugee in Spino Bianco area, and for Peppino whose wife and daughter were at Borgo Montello, they were far from their families but they nevertheless preferred to stay with the people of Nettuno. There was room for everyone in the huts and farmsteads of the evacuees. It seemed impossible that so many dozens of people could manage to live together in a few square meters. It was another miracles belonging to the poor, traditionally resourceful in their lot as peasants and fishing folks: the spirit of adaptation, that is, the ability to scrape a living from stones and rocks, which is here a simple gesture like the sowing of the grain and the pulling in of the nets.

A word with an archaic flavor to it, "rapazzuola", meaning a pallet, or shakedown, is still used in the language of the people of Nettuno even today, and it gives an idea of the whole situation. It has nothing to do with the turnips (rape) from which it might be thought to be derived, and as proof of its twin habitat, it belongs as much to the shepherd as to the sailor. The 'rapazzuola' on board a boat, means the simplest bunk of all, that of the cabin-boy; in the huts in the country it is big straw pallet, usually stuffed with maize leaves, placed on top boards with smaller planks laid crossing and propped up by another pieces of wood.

On this plank bed, which seems complicated from the description but is in fact easy to assemble and take apart, whole families slept, and it proved to be a generous bed also for the 'Carabinieri' of the Nettuno Station. Sgt. Pitruzzello and his deputy, Di Iorio, friends of Giovanni Monaco, known as Nino, were hidden in the latter's vineyard, at Zucchetti area. In October, following the second order by the Germans to evacuate, they were forced to move further away. Nino again found the solution, with the help of kind Elvira Passa who put a tumbledown hut at their disposal at Piscina Cardillo.

Nino, who was then owner of a newsagent and tobacconist shop (the one beside the arch in Via del Quartiere), had been forced to separate from his wife and children, when they were evacuated to Pomezia. He still had with him, as a refuge, a fifteen years boy, Adriano Birzi, who was worth much more than the usual shop-boy, he could cope with the intricacies of all his business, from running the stall to hawking papers in the Piazza, to helping in the grape-harvest. No longer a newsvendor, Adriano had retired to the porter's cubby hole in a building in Via Napoli. His memory had remained blocked at the point in which he saw Sgt. Pitruzzello die because of a misunderstanding, like the one which killed the car-hire man from Otricoli.

The story is something of a tangle, with more than one obscure point. No-one ever know how the sergeant managed to enter into contact with the Germans and make a deal with them. In any case, it was the needs of the population which drove him to it; scattered all over the countryside, it was always a mob to be kept in order. So for a start, the distribution of bread needed to be carried out without confusion. And it cannot be said that everything was clear about infiltrators. There were shady characters around, who caused a lot of anxiety, especially to the women, because every day news came from the town partially (and conveniently) justifying the shooting – about thefts from apartments left unguarded. And so, in the first days of December, there was Pitruzzello back in uniform.

To the Germans, it perhaps did not seem true that, after the civic policeman, also the 'Carabinieri' should be resuming their service on their own initiative, and committing themselves to the maintenance of good conduct amongst the refugees. The sergeant tried to keep well away from the German command post in Piazza Mazzini, and having called Di Iorio and the others to join him, he led them to the Convent of the Casa del Sole, in the old slaughter-house quarter, where also was the anti-aircraft shelter. The nuns had left, and the home of a religious community must have seemed to them more independent, as a barracks. Moreover, it enabled him to return Nino's hospitality since he could keep a room there for him and one for Adriano. At 10 o'clock on the morning of the landing, two Italian-American parachutists appeared at the Casa del Sole, armed with sub-machine-guns. They knew everything, but only up to a point. For them, the eight 'Carabinieri', plus the two in civilian clothes, were collaborators. They asked them: "Are you fascists?". "We are soldiers of the King", replied the 'Carabinieri'. But they arrested them just the same, and were clever enough on their own, to march them off, all together, along the road to the Piave Barracks.

Half way along the hill the sound of a machine gun fire, in the Brovelli brothers' olive grove to their left sent them scattering. Some here, some there, they gathered under the plane-trees. Monaco was the first to realize that over the other side it was not the Germans, but other Americans, and he yelled to the two parachutists to identify themselves. The only reply was another round of fire. Pitruzzello said to Monaco: "We can't stay here like this. I am going!", and he jumped out at once, followed by Di Iorio.

He only took a few steps. Perhaps he really believed that for him and the others there was no chance but in flight by way of the shortcut through the caves. Or perhaps, more than the fear of being compromised with the Germans, he was spurred by the thought that he would have to give an account of his behavior. He was hit in the abdomen, and died slowly. His ever faithful lance-sergeant, injured by the volley, managed to recover thanks to the ministrations of the Donati brothers. "The real misunderstanding arose because there

ANZIO-NETTUNO BEACH HEAD

were ten of us and only two paratroopers". Adriano said nothing else.

For him, a boy among men, it was a trauma. Pitruzzello, was buried in Nettuno, inscription on his tomb read: "Tragically died at 38 years with the radiant vision before him of a liberated Italy" the words of his friend Giovanni Monaco. Indeed more than that was needed that morning to cloud the skies again for the people of Nettuno and Anzio. How could those rays of sunshine be doubted? The Germans had gone, and the Americans were there, right before their eyes, with chocolate, Camels, chewing gum; maybe they could even put together a band for some boogie-woogie. The evacuees came running from all over the place, and more than one of them dragged out a demijohn of wine to offer them. It was the cry everywhere: "We are free, we are free! The war is over. Long live the liberators".

For days later, four children, Anna, Iole, Sergio and Luciano, belonging to the numerous family of Armando Ottaviani, left their hut at Piscina Cardillo and came on foot to Nettuno. They had laft behind on the palled-bed, in the arms of their tearful mother, two others: Stefano, was only a few months old and Rosanna, who was two. The mother was desperate, because Armando and her eldest son Eugenio had already gone to meet the

Americans and already not been seen or heard of since.

They were assumed killed, by the mines. In order to get further news of them, Anna, Iole, Sergio and Luciano walked for hours, right through the hundreds of soldiers, hundreds of jeeps and hundreds of other things, without anyone taking any notice of them. When they arrived at their home – which was in the space which is now both the road for St. Giacomo district and the main road to the American cemetery – it was evening. They saw lights in the windows and at once they hoped that they had found their father and brother. However, it was an American sergeant who opened the door to them. They remained open-mouthed, speechless. What was he doing there? What happened? How could they explain that that kitchen, that short corridor and the bathroom and those little bedrooms were theirs?

The sergeant realized at once what he had to do, and he took the children by the hand and led them to the nearest cave. This was the quarry of the Martinis and here they learned from other Nettuno people that Eugenio and his father had gone to work with the Americans and were safe and sound. However, they couldn't get any sleep, because the guns were thundering all night, and they had to stop their ears against the explosions and the pressure waves. The Germans had come back and were making themselves heard.

ANZIO-NETTUNO BEACH HEAD

An ancient statue of a woman with an helmet on her head, stands in a landing ship as a trophy. The American used to call her "Anzio Annie", like the big 280 mm. railway gun.

ANZIO-NETTUNO BEACH HEAD

26 January 1944 – Cpt. Frederick J. Saam, of the 1st Ranger Bn. Hdq. holds old Roman helmet and fancy walking stick found in the ruins of Anzio.

Louis Michielini and two other soldiers of the OSS - Office of Strategic Service - fight as ancient warriors in the Sangallo Fortress.

THE BREAK-OUT AND THE HOMECOMING

To the losses incurred by the Rangers there were added those, equally serious of the British 1st Division. Supported by Harmon's tanks, they had reached Campoleone Station, but with such a slender salient that they could nor defend it. By now the Germans were surrounding the beachhead. They began their attack on 3rd February, wiping out the salient. They retook Aprilia and from there and from Carroceto, on 16th February, unleashed the offensive that – according to Hitler, who was directing it from Germany – should have thrown the Allies back into the sea within three days. The Allies, pushed in the direction of Anzio, got into trouble between the flyover bridge at Campo di Carne and the Padiglione tower. They were on the verge of disaster but nevertheless reacted in such a way that the enemy, now being subjected to massive aerial bombardments was halted definitively. Hitler demanded that Kesserling and Mackensen make another attempt to break through on the Cisterna side, but that was soon quashed by the Americans. By the 1st March the German forces were exhausted. From then on the armies remained facing one another, until the

ANZIO-NETTUNO BEACH HEAD

Allies returned to the attack – from 23rd to the 26th May. The 6th Corps, encouraged by the fall of Cassino, broke the siege at Cisterna and at last, they could join up with General Clark's divisions on their way to take Rome. Once the war had taken itself off, the Nettuno and Anzio people who had evacuated to southern Italy, were able to come back home, together with the Madonna of Grace.

NO PARACHUTES

One of the greatest sources of fury of Churchill was over the paratroops, as he made clear in the letter to Smuts on 27 February, from which we quoted previously. Taking up cudgels with the Americans, he makes his accusation as follow: "In all his talks with me, Alexander envisaged the essence of the battle was the seizure of the Alban Hills with the utmost speed. And to this end I was able to obtain from the United States their 504th Parachute Regiment, although at the time it was under orders to return for 'Overlord'. But at the last moment General Clark cancelled the use of this regiment... (Churchill, *Op. cit.* p.436).

And this was the second misunderstanding. The first if we may be excused for repeating ourselves, took place in Naples over the directives issued by Alexander for the landing, and interpreted by Clark in his own way, when he suggested to Lucas the he should act differently. There was also to e a third, indicating that relations between partners are apt to be difficult when there are differing viewpoints. If they were equals, discussions are never-ending; if they are not, then it is rare for the stronger partner, even though he may be wrong, to give way to the opinion of the other. It is no coincidence that when he refers to the Teheran Conference Churchill is careful to record two of Stalin's unfriendly interventions. Certainly Stalin was adept at putting his finger on, or making his interlocutors put their finger on, awkward questions and then pretending that they weren't awkward at all.

'Uncle Joe' as both the Prime Minister and Roosevelt called him in their correspondence heartily disliked General Alan Brooke, the Chief of Imperial General Staff who was headed by Churchill more than any of his other advisers. This was partly because, despite his aristocratic appearance and his studies on bird life, he was in fact Churchill's fighting-cock in his dialectical battles with the Allies. It was Brooke, with his objections, who had enraged the Americans at the Cairo summit on 23rd November, and he only just avoided being punched by Admiral Ernest King. The same objections had caused considerable irritation to the Russian during their first encounter in Moscow more than a year earlier.

When he saw him again at Teheran, Stalin never ceased to give him dirty looks, and he took advantage of a lunch offered by Churchill for his own birthday – 30th November – to fire a direct broadside at the general, just at the moment when the toasts were being made:

-You have failed to show real feeling of friendship towards the Red Army. I hope in future you'll be able to show greater comradeship towards our soldiers.
-The accusations against me are entirely unfounded. You have a wrong notion of what I'm like.
-If that's so, don't get upset. The best friendship are those founded on misunderstanding.
Amidst misunderstanding, the goal opportunity of Anzio-Nettuno nearly became the auto-goal of the Allies. In all the tragedy, the responsibilities for the war, can we absolve those who provoked those misunderstanding, or did too little to avoid them? Of course, Stalin's case, the question of conscience doesn't even arise. Churchill, who had pleaded the cause of Finland, didn't take umbrage at the replay he received from him: "After all, allies could squeeze each other if they wanted to from time to time". (Churchill, *Op. cit.*, p. 353).
And so it was the affair of the American parachutists. However, it would be quite unjust and his historically false to explain it by giving an impression of Roosevelt as arrogant. On the contrary; in fact, far from abusing the strength of his own position, he treated Churchill with every respect in the direction of the war. For better or for worse, through his most trusted adviser Marshall,

it was the President of the US himself who decided to act as a mediator between the plans of the American High Command and the requests of the British Prime Minister; and it was he who refused to turn down Operation Shingle, and obtain the use of the paratroops for it. Up till the last minute, Alexander had been afraid that he might be forced to renounce it all.

It is here that the strategist we already know emerges again. For someone like Churchill who was by no means rash, but was not, either, so cautions as to fear running a few risks, the airborne troops and the marine commandos were ideal for the surprise attacks. In fact, when he could do nothing but complain, and wrote that he had envisaged "a wild cat, not a great whale stranded on the shore" of Anzio-Nettuno, it was not a matter of being wise after the event. His wild cat, given the limits of the 6th Corps, also included dropping armed men from the sky especially to immobilize the enemy and get Clark and Lucas moving.

With this end in view, even the exchange of New Year greetings was for Churchill a pretext to remind Roosevelt that the settling of accounts was near. His card thanking him for his Christmas presents ended with a message which was not exactly that of Bethlehem: "Alexander reports he has arranged satisfactory plans with Clark for Anzio. He is using the British 1st and the American 3rd Divisions, with paratroops and armor. I am glad of this. It is fitting that we should share equally in suffering, risk and honor". (Churchill, *Op, cit,* p. 394).

But a few days later came the hitch. Alexander, who perhaps, secretly, was not all that put out, telegrammed to the Prime Minister that other difficulties had arisen because of the second thoughts of Marshall's staff, who were preparing to withdraw the 504th Parachute Regiment from Italy. This was an insurmountable difficulty for Alexander, since he had nothing at hand with which to replace the American regiment, while Eisenhower, who at that moment was back in the USA, held that it was not the right moment to insist that they should be made available.

Churchill, on the other hand, was absolutely insistent. He followed his general's note then doing the rounds of Washington with his own by no means submissive plea: "Eisenhower is now with Marshall. Will you appeal to them to let this 504th American Regiment do this one fine and critical job before they come back home for 'Overlord'? It is so rarely that opportunities for decisive air action by paratroops present themselves, and it seems improvident to take them from the decisive point just when they might render exemplary and outstanding service". (Churchill, *Op. cit.* p. 392).

Roosevelt was unable to say no. But the use that was made of the 504th Regiment – loaded on to the ships, landed behind the 3rd Division of Truscott, and actually held as a reserve corps – meant to Churchill what Stalin had said: a squeeze. It was one of the most disputed questions at the end of the war. Between those for a those against, it seemed to Clark that he was in the middle of a heated sporting argument about the previous day's match. In his Monday inquest he defended himself like a coach accused of having produced the wrong team. He had had to abandon the idea of dropping the parachutists – so the official war history published in Washington says – because if he had sent them in prior to the landing, it would have served as a warning to the Germans of the package that was about to be delivered, and if he had allowed them to drop at the same time as the landing, the long-range guns could have caught them as they dropped.

In defense of Clark, one can quote one of the many friends the Nettuno-Anzio people – as though humanity was compensating them for their wounds – acquired as a result of the war. He is Louis A. Hauptfleisch, then a 1st Lt. and later a Cpt.

and a adjutant to Colonel Reuben H. Tucker, who was in command of the 504th Regiment at Salerno, at Nettuno and in Germany. Louis, who came originally from Illinois, has settled in a small town in New Jersey, on the bank of the Passaic. It bears an auspicious name: Summit. "The best thing in New Jersey, he says, is a little place that you people from Nettuno ought to know about: its name is Nettuno, just like your own town Nettuno, though we call it Neptune. And the actor Jack Nicholson was born there. But for those of us who were in the 504th, the name of Neptune has quite another importance.

Louis was over 70 then. He had left the army in 1945, on Christmas Eve, and was a bank cashier till 1983. After his retirement he had plenty of time to devote to the historical archives and publications of the regiment. As part of the 82nd Airborne Division, had his headquarters at Fort Bragg in North Carolina. In his war diary two dates stand out: 13th September 1943, relating to the drop on Salerno four days after Clark's landing, and the 17th September one year later, when he and his comrades were dropped in Holland in the aftermath of 'Overlord'.

-Why did Clark decide at the last minute, as Wilson has made clear, that the 504th should not take off from the ground at Nettuno-Anzio? (This is the

ANZIO-NETTUNO BEACH HEAD

first question we asked him in our telephone interview).

"We had never understood that we were supposed to be doing a drop on 22nd January. An operation of that kind can't be improvised. Don't forget that we were really always a mere infantry regiment".

-What does it means?

"It means something different from the selected parachute divisions, which had genuine athletes and special weapons. For what Churchill had in mind, many days of training were essential, and suitable equipment. Instead, without even putting us through a practice drop, the Command of the Fifth Army allowed us to spend our rest-time quietly at Pozzuoli, where we stayed through half of December after having fought at Salerno, Naples and then at Venafro, between Isernia and Cassino".

-How many were you? Could your regiment have altered the situation radically if you'd been dropped?

"There was a chance for us to do a good job. And we could have made the Germans recovery more difficult; but from that to taking the Alban Hills, not to mention liberating Rome itself, would have been a huge leap. We were not more than 2000, divided into three battalions. Another element to keep in mind is that before the Normandy landing on the night of the 5th- 6th June 1944, three whole divisions of parachutists were dropped.

-There was another paratroop battalion with you, the 509th.

"It wasn't part of our division. They came from Avellino, and were commanded by Lt. Col. William P. Yarborough. Independent and autonomous like all the special units, they were placed alongside the Rangers in the first wave of landings".

-But both Salerno and in Holland, you were dropped after the landing had taken place. Could the same thing have been done in our case?

"With the forces which were mobilized in Naples, it wasn't possible to make a drop, neither before nor after, It would have had to be done some hours earlier, as in Normandy. This would have involved modifying the timetable, and thus complications for the fleet as well, and even more than the paratroops, the fleet needed the night to provide it with cover. From Naples to Anzio is not like crossing the Channel, And then – detail which always seems to be forgotten – there weren't enough planes to transport the regiment, which would have had to be accompanied by at least fifty gliders loaded with armored cars and anti-tank guns, and there was not even an airbase in the area which would have been suitable for the operation. We might have been able to manage with the one at Foggia, but as I said, there weren't enough planes anyway".

This had to be taken into account. Trevelyan, for instance, who is quite critical of the Allied generals, is nevertheless among those who produce evidence to support the case for the defense: "The reason given for the cancellation of the air-drop were many, including one blamed on General Penney, who thought that as the drop would be near the Flyover, in the British sector, there would be a risk of mistaking American helmets and uniforms for the German equivalent". (Trevelyan, *Op. cit.* p. 81).

There were never enough precautions against this type of incident, all too common in the battlefield. Clark had discovered this for himself. He had spent a bad quarter of an hour during one of his excursion from the mouth of the Volturno to the landing zone, on the 28th January: the torpedo boat PT 201, in which he was travelling, was mistaken for a German boat and had no time to identify itself and was hit by grenades from the American minesweeper AM 120. There were casualties, both killed and wounded. The commander of the Fifth Army, thrown off his seat, escaped unscathed.

However, he could hardly avoid coming off badly in the polemic about the paratroops Let us forget the Monday inquest. Knowing whether the 504th Regiment should or should not have been parachuted (assuming there are still some doubts) is only interesting up to as point. The unpardonable fact is that when the program was changed in extremis (or rather not changed because the possibility of a drop had never even been taken into serious consideration) no-one had thought it his duty to let Churchill know. According to his own account, he was very perturbed, and had had to wire General Wilson on 6th February for an explanation: "Why was the 504th Regiment of paratroops not used at Anzio as proposed?".

However, at this point, Churchill's own behavior doesn't exactly throw light on the matter, and it seems indeed that he was the one who kept all the questions alive as they grew more and more disquieting, rather like the introduction to a documentary film. Wilson's replay could not have been delayed, and one would have imagined it to be precise and exhaustive. Instead, he replied to his chief with only two lines: "The 504th was seaborne and not airborne because that was what General Clark decided at the last minute".

This was all we can find in Churchill's books. He took the blow, and that was that. It's not something we would have expected of him, that he would have allowed himself to be set aside so brusquely, after preparing for a serious investigation, not just a trivia quiz. It seems almost certain that he did not wish to take the lid off the saucepan. Why? Was the main reason to avoid launching a ferocious attack on Clark, and let the reader rather draw his own conclusion? Or was it a matter of closing not just one but both eyes at Alexander's negligence, since he was standing at Clark's elbow, after all, and could hardly have avoided knowing what his intentions were, besides demanding to be informed of all details regarding the landing plan? Was it that the baronet, like the Prime Minister was merely misinformed?

Another question follows: Why did Churchill, no longer in the dark about the paratroops waiting idle in the ships, from which they disembarked at midday on 22nd January, remain silent for two weeks, and make a protest only after things had gone wrong? Perhaps he was not all that sure of himself, and he may well have reflected in this way: "Who knows whether the Americans may not have been right to be so careful? Let's stay and watch, and see what happens".

What happened was the end of the world. A few hours after the lost battle at Cisterna and Campoleone, a dispatch from General Wilson had been set down on Churchill's desk; it presented a black present and an even blacker future: "The beach-head is surrounded and our forces inside it are no longer able to advance". It was immediately clear in London and Washington that Lucas and his men had ended up in the quicksand, and were at risk of sinking. Churchill, who then took on the role of inquisitor, didn't confine his enquiries to the parachutists. He demanded an inventory of the goods, and the count of everything: how many lorries, how many drivers, how many mechanics, how many odd-job men were crowded in there at Nettuno-Anzio, without serving any purpose for the front-line?

A report came back from this which was like a woodworm in the ear for Marshall and his collaborators, who began to suspect that something shady had undermined their team's success, rather in the way that a team fans were when, after keeping the lead in the football Trophy for nearly the whole season, they were finally forced to hand it over to another team. The inquire by the American Chief of Staff was greeted by Churchill with an utterance like that of Public Prosecutor: "I am, in fact, by no means surprised". Even Lucas, who was not contentious, in this predicament took his side. In terms of strategy, especially considering the outcome of his belated sortie, he could hardly do other than share the

Prime Minister's regrets at the failure to make use of the 504th Regiment. More specifically, "Lucas admitted that the presence of these paratroopers half-way to Campoleone, might have given him an incentive to join up with them on the first day". (Trevelyan, *Op. cit*. p.82).

What were the conclusions of the American enquiry? Once again silence on the part of Churchill. It is very odd. However, there is no doubt that excuses were due, and it may be that someone hastened to make them, at least verbally. Fair play above all else, especially if one is a member of a team. The people of Nettuno-Anzio, when they collect the apples, always say: "It's as well to know how to lie in the basket".

Let's take another look at the house where General Lucas lived in Nettuno. You already have the address. It is a two-storey building, with a garden and two palm-tree in front. It belonged to Domenico Combi; his daughter Laura fitted it out as a small hotel after the war, with a neon sign reading 'Pensione Villa delle Palme' in an arc over the entrance-gate. It must in fact have had many of the requirements for a good boarding-house, including a cellar in which to shelter from the bombardments, since it had also been chosen by Lt. Querbach, the commander of the German Garrison. (He had been forced to go without warning and all that was left of him was the remains of his last supper in Nettuno: a piece of sausage and a glass of white wine, hardly touched.) Later on, the villa was sold and rebuilt; replaced by a four-storey building. Even the Piazza del Mercato, the market place is no longer the same. It is here that Clark came to decorate the bravest of the men all standing on their feet, and the Stars and Stripes flying as if it were in some corner of the Pentagon at Arlington. The sea god has gone, along with the fountain-basin, to preside over Piazza Mazzini, leaving behind two pipes which continue to pour water from a fragment of the old monument. Opposite, the palms still survive, much taller, no doubt, but much drier than the one Lucas knew.

From here to Via Romana, where the headquarters was moved from the Donati barracks, after the Stukas airplanes' attack on 7th February, at the 'Osteria dell'artigliere' which became the operation centre of the 6th Corps, Lucas only had to walk a few yards. Their command room was in the ground-floor with all the offices in the underground; and that of the Military Police was in the next building where the Padiglione and La Villetta restaurants used to be before the German occupation. For Lucas's convenience a dining-room had also been installed on the ground-floor of Benedetto Fedeli's little villa on the right of Via Romana. This was a strictly private dining-room, for a few intimate friends, where only the leaders were admitted. It was there that Lucas welcomed Alexander and Clark, when they came to visit and congratulate him three days after the landing.

Emma Gatti has preserved an unforgettable impression of Alexander, with his black jacket which he removed before coming into the dining-room. One might say that as she watched him coming – agile, lean, thin-faced . across the little court-yard of the villa, she had already committed his portrait to memory. Her husband, Riccardo Gatti, was the adopted son of Benedetto Fedeli and mayor of Nettuno from 1956 to 1958. Emma Gatti was a painter and a potter and, like Novella Parigini of Via Margutta, in Rome, she was determinate to make a name with her drawings of cats (which is the translation in English of the surname Gatti). No-one enjoyed more favor than she did among the Allied officers, they would take their photographs of their mothers, wives, and children from their wallets and beg her to make oil paintings to hang in their rooms.

However, for Lucas and his tablemates, Emma was primarily a great cook. Every day she went back and forth to the cave – there was less and less light for painting. Via Romana has also become one of the targets for the night attacks of Stukas airplanes, so accurately timed and planned that people were beginning to bet that either fascists or spies placed by the Germans were guiding them from the ground, with light signals. In March, on the night of St. Giuseppe, when Lucas had already had hand over everything to Truscott, the bomb fell a few stores away. The food store was destroyed, and it was there that Corporal Kammerlocher died; he had been called in by the Allies in February to take the guard-post over from Zecchinelli. In the great confusion, the first concern was to close the general dining-room.

Emma had always taken care of it. She was in charge of the kitchen and not only because of her easy relations with Lucas and his companions (it often happened, for instance, that the perfectly mannered Gregson-Ellis, the commander of the 5th British Division, accompanied the cook and her helper to the cave before sitting down to eat). As well as her flair for colors, she had a flair for gastronomy and therefore the menu was left to her, even though there was not a great deal to inspire the imagination in tinned food from the American army stores. In preparing the food, however, she needed the help of her sister-in-law, Rosina Ottolini (who, even since the bakery in Via Carlo Cattaneo had been reopened had seen to it that there was a supply of fresh bread) and, above all, the strong arm of Quinta, the wife of Nello Venditti the pastry chef. With flour and powered eggs, the latter rolled off her pastry board noodles that had Alexander liking his fingers.

The commander of the 6th Corps was to be ingloriously disposed of, as though he had conducted his entire mission from this very short stretch of road, Piazza del Mercato to Via Romana and back. His accuser, almost all of them English, were ruthless. It was symptomatic that right from the start their principal spokesman concerning the Anzio-Nettuno front. William Ronald Cambell Penney, had always criticized Lucas. Despite this, Lucas did not allow himself to be caught on the hop when Alexander and Clark made their on-the-spot inspection a few hours after the landing. He had in fact accompanied them on their inspection, he had showed them the troops under the command, and had agreed with them what was to be done, When he learned of the contretemps with the British, who had been caught unawares by the mines, he had immediately taken a boat to go and confer with Penney, who was on board of the 'Bulolo'. However, as if to suggest absenteeism, it was noted that on 22nd January, Lucas had not disembarked; that he waited until the next day, that he decided to leave the 'Biscayne', where he had shared a cabin with Truscott, and go and shut himself up in his cellar in Nettuno. For the sake of truth, we quote the book 'Command Mission' writer by Lucien K. Truscott who wrote in his memories that in the morning of 22nd January, at his command post in the Foglino woods,

at about 11 am, Lucas and his collaborators of the 6th Corps, after returned from the inspection to the British sector, joined him for breakfast along with the generals: Clark, Don Brann, Donovan; about the absenteeism and shut himself in the cellar of Nettuno, this is untrue: Lucas' first headquarters was in the artillery barracks in Via St. Maria N. 39 (near to Piazza del Mercato) and he moved to the 'Osteria dell'artigliere' after Stukas airplanes' attack of 7th February, and his office was in the ground-floor ; for safety of all the men who were on service for 6th Corps, the Canadian's engineers made the underground cellars connected one to another and available to use them as offices.

But there were also several English soldiers in the cellars. Among these, the one closest to the commander was an officer of the Scots Guards, Major John Hope – in reality Lord John. The son of a marquis, it was evident that he had been to Eton college. This distinction contrasted with the corn-cob pipe which characterized the Virginia Lucas, a native of Kearneysville. Hope says that he had immediately liked the ruddy countrified countenance of the American. He showed it in his own way, giving him confidence such as he probably never received.

One, on the 24th January he had limited himself to watching in silence. Lucas never stopped poring over the maps. All of a sudden, in a voice which must have been stentorian, he said: "Lookee, Hope, I sure am going to attack. But what am I to attack? What would you attack?". "Sir", replied Hope, "why don't you send a patrol up the Alban road and see what's happening?". "Well, I might as well do that. Hell, I want to attack". (Trevelyan, *Op. cit.* p.73). (For the sake of truth, even in this case, Lucas was waiting the arrive of Harmon's 1st Armored Division, which landing was completed on 29th January; and after that he felt ready to attack, but it was too late).

Another time, since Lucas was elaborating and examining the plans, and approving them even when they were mistaken (as happened in the case of the Rangers who were wiped out at Cisterna), what did the mannered Lord do? Precisely nothing. He claimed that he was looking to say: "Why don't you go up to the front and see for yourself?" (Trevelyan, *Op. cit.* p. 82).

The truth is that Lucas needed a bulldozer to get moving. It was very rare for his jeep to venture on longer journey than the twenty-minute one from one terminus to another which the bus service now makes from Nettuno to the harbor of Anzio, to which, in his impatience to sight and welcome reinforcements, he was constantly attracted. During his first visit, Alexander accompanied him and stayed with him to watch the operations of unloading the Liberty, congratulating him with the words: "Very well".

In the circumstances, his comment should have been extended to the group if Italians who, like Capt. Pezzella's 'Carabinieri', had arrived from Pozzuoli, about a hundred and fifty in all. These were volunteers, recruited from among the people taking refuge at Battipaglia. This had become an open camp, without fences, for refugees and people made homeless after the 6th September. They had entered any door and were camping as best as they could with tents and burned-out vehicles. An Italian-American, Sgt. Savino, had convinced them, since manpower was running short, to join the 66th Company and register for arms and munitions. Thus for more than two months, for the pay of a dollar a day, equivalent to 100 Am-liras, they had followed the Fifth Army and as fatigue troops had slogged hard at Maddaloni, Venafro and Teano.

They were sent urgently to the beach-head because they were just the people needed to empty the ships moored to the jetty or anchored outside the port. They were unarmed though wearing American uniform. They could be distinguished by a badge in the design of a boot, sewn on their left sleeves. The majority were from Rome, from Umbria Region, or Toscana, several were from the city of Frosinone and there was even one man from Milan. They were hoping to rejoin their families as soon as possible. Among them, Umberto Coppola, Marco Ambrosini and Vittorio Bergami, all three from Anzio, had already drunk a health to the return on the Pozzuoli quay.

They were greeted by a great pile of rubble and bulldozers trying to open the way from the harbor and from Piazza Pia through to the Nettunense highway and to the coastal road. The devastation, the dust, and then the sudden vision of the ruined town, made another Anzio man, Lucio Castaldi, close his eyes. He was attached to the 57th Battalion of the US 3rd Division, and had landed at Foglino woods, twenty-four hours earlier. The families of Marco and Vittorio had been evacuated to Rome. Umberto took fifteen days to locale his; in their search for safety, they could hardly chosen a more dangerous place: the Moletta ditch, which was destined to be filled with blood. His mother,

ANZIO-NETTUNO BEACH HEAD

Annunziata Valle, his wife, four children, his brother Vittorio and his sister Gina with three children, together with their few remaining pieces of furniture, formed caravan that Umberto managed to get away in time. They all then squeezed into an improvised hut on the small patch of land he owned in Nettuno, beyond the Piave barracks, now the site of the new sport center.

For him, Vittorio, Marco and the other port unloaders, their dormitory was further off. They had to dig one out for themselves, using picks and shovels, in the field of the Campana and Piscina Cardillo. The storehouse of the 66th Company was situated there. But they were used to the job by now and, pocking their way into the ditches and covering themselves with planks, had learned to live with the bomb-cases. On the evening of the 23rd January they arrived in large Piazza della Divina Provvidenza and saw paratroops of the 509th pushing along five or six ragged Germans whom they had dug out of an outhouse of the military Garrison building. This made them feel more at home, and they hadn't the slightest inkling of the impending apocalypse.

Lucas, on the contrary, always felt it bearing down on him. So why, we may ask, did he take no notice, in his office in the artillery barracks of Via St.

Maria of the wise advice, unspoken but surely discernible, implied, of Major Hope? But we may also ask whether it would have sufficed. We don't say it would have overcome the original mistakes, the half-heartedness of the fate of Operation Shingle, but at least it would have saved him from disgrace and allowed him to live a little longer; the torment of the wrong he had suffered, more than the humiliation itself, would drive him to his grave in 1949. Going through it all again with a tooth-comb, and rereading material that has been filed away, the truth emerges and it is certain that he greatest responsibility for the four months of Calvary which Anzio and Nettuno went through lies with others: Lucas had to pay the price for all of them.

He was well aware of it. His subsequent judgments spared no-one. He wrote of Churchill and Alexander that "the ignorance of military matters shown by the leaders of people who had been at war for such a long time" left him dumbfounded, He wrote that everything had been organized in haste and badly done, and that given another week it would have been possible "to save dozens of lives. But the order came from the civilian minister of another country who impatiently set aside details of that kinds".

This is letting off steam. With the convictions, as we've already said, Lucas should have refused to take the command of the 6th Corps. The fact that he goes on to quote Patton, who had given him his blessing before he left for Anzio-Nettuno: "John, there's no-one in the army I'd hate to see get killed as much as you, but you can't get out of this alive", only goes to show that even the man who wanted to "save dozens of lives" didn't do enough to save them. Which doesn't alter the fact that he was condemned unjustly and was not able to rejoice in the final victory like any other American.

For the record it should be stated that he did put in some appearances at the front, when it was a matter of putting his foot down. Cpt. Nicholas S. Mansell, a great lover of Italy who fell near Campo di Carne while he was leaping out a trench, described the event in his diary: "A real flurry. Would you believe it? Old Corncob Charlie has actually been near here to see Penney...". But what did Penney get out it? "No operational appreciation, he wrote afterwards, no orders, no objective, no nothing". This is an exaggeration: General Clark, even though belatedly and with a heavy conscience, has re-established the truth: "Penney was beginning to itch at poor Lucas. Lucas knew he was being sniped at. He knew the

British were going to get him, and they did. They ganged up on him". (Trevelyan, *Op.cit.* pp. 82-83). It was Alexander who made the decisive move, on 15th February, the very day on which the Montecassino Abbey was destroyed. Among other things, the rapid turn of events at the beach-head, with Lucas and his army in the last ditch, and the Allies' urgent need for a diversion which would cause Kesserling to loosen his grip, has been considered one of the justifications for the terrible bombardment. Let us say at once that Alexander made sure not to attribute this, at least, to Lucas. But after having said more than once that he was "the best of the American generals", he really scalped him when he wrote to his own Minister of War as follows: "I am disappointed in the commander of the 6th Corps. He is inactive, and lacks the energy and enthusiasm necessary to carry out his task. It would seem that he has been overcome by events. What is needed is a bold and decisive man like George Patton aided by a competent general staff. Or the whole leadership of the 6th Corps should be replaced by an English commander and general staff. The second solution may seem to be very drastic, but I would like to know from Eisenhower what reaction it would provoke, in his opinion". (Trevelyan, *Op. cit.* p. 162).

The reaction was this. Alan Brooke replied to Alexander that he should forget any notion of an English take-over of the controls. Only as an emergency measure, he added: "Eisenhower would be prepared to spare Patton for a month, but his personal selection for a replacement for Lucas would be: 1 – Truscott; 2 – Eagles; 3 – Harmon". (Trevelyan, *Op. cit.* p. 162). The was open, an d that was the direction which would have to be taken. The intervention with which Alexander managed to get through Clark's defenses at this juncture has been taken as an example of diplomacy: "You know, the situation is really grave. We run the risk of being thrown back into the sea. It would be a quite serious affair for both of us, and you would certainly be relieved of your command". (Alexander, *The Alexander Memoirs,* p. 156).
Clark yielded to this threat, described by Alexander himself as a "gentle injunction". What was he to do: fire Lucas or be fired in his place? The same Clark, who had no vocation to martyrdom, didn't spend much time in Hamlet-like indecision, either. He acted step by step. On 17th February he ordered in a communiqué that Truscott should hand over the command of the 3rd Division to John W. O'Daniel, and become Lucas' deputy, together with the English General Vyvyan

Evelegh, five days later, he came in person to Anzio-Nettuno, and at 8:00 p.m. seated at his table in his office at Prince Steno Borghese's villa, where the Fifth Army Advance Headquarters had been established since 6th February, put it to Lucas: "I'm sorry. Try to understand. I can't hold out any longer against Alexander and Devers. They say you're tired. I have to replace you". (Clark, *Calculated Risk*, p. 299).

Lucas replay was: "We're all tired". He left Anzio-Nettuno the following day. When Clark promoted Truscott he had indicated that he would be taking Lucas to Presenzano, below Cassino, as his second-in-command. And it happened for a few weeks. While at Presenzano Clark decorated Lucas with a Silver Star, for Operation Shingle. After that Lucas was given three weeks' rest in Sorrento and then sent home. As consolation prize he was given command of the 4th Army, a kind of territorial army maintained in the United States.

From that moment Clark never got tired of defending himself and made use of every opportunity to raise his hat to his courageous comrade in arms: "It was my impression that Johnny Lucas was feeling the strain, both physically and mentally, of the continuing responsibility under fire. He died a few years later. I have never intended to do anything that would harm the man who contributed so much to our success from Salerno upwards". (Clark, *Calculated Risk*, p. 299).

And what about Lucas himself? He had not been surprised by Alexander's ostracizing. On this regards it is useful to read what we have known from Alan Brooke's book, about Alexander. After the war General Alexander in his *Dispatches* wrote: "At the time of the landing I thought that Lucas was wrong, but reconsidering the situation he realized that he did it well in consolidate the beach-head and wait". (Alan Brooke, *War Diaries, chapter Flames on the Mediterranean*, p. 282).

Lucas suffered more from the below-the-belt blow by his fellow-American Jacob L. Devers. This was something he wasn't expecting. Barely a week earlier, the Deputy Commander in the Mediterranean had come to Anzio-Nettuno to confirm his faith in him, and nothing had been said to give any warning about a change of heart. Even Clark might have re-read the message which he sent immediately on hearing the news that the American tanks had definitely beaten back the Germans. The text ran: "Congratulate Harmon on his success. I want to tell you again that the results you have obtained today are excellent. Keep up the good work". It had deceived Lucas: "I thought I was winning something of a victory".

It was nothing less than dismissal. Lucas left the scene with his head held high: "I left the finest soldiers in the world when I lost the 6th Corps, and the honor of having commanded them in their hour of greatest travail cannot be taken from me". Apart from the military honor, something else which belongs to him is one of the two palm trees at No. 16/A in Piazza del Mercato, which have ended up in recent years with their crowns above the level of the roof. His is the taller of the two: it stands for honesty, which on 31st January, after the disaster with the Rangers, led him to admit: "...Clark blames Truscott. He says that they were used foolishly... Neither I nor Truscott knew of the organized defensive position they would run into. I told Clark that the fault was mine as I had seen the plan of the attack and had OK'd it". No-one has ever called his honesty into question.

Just as in unending conflicts between mother-in-law and daughter-in-law, Lucas himself was lacking in the spirit of reconciliation. The English accused him of this, concerned as they were to demonstrate that they didn't bring him down because of prejudice or malice. They point the finger at him first of all for the conduct of the war, but their hostility may well also have been provoked by his own statements, which as they have been reported were not designed to pacify them or produce an atmosphere of love and harmony! Lucas would have preferred an all-Yankee army, and not the "hermaphrodite" one (his expression was obviously meant to refer to the fifty-fifty nature of the landing corps, not to its being male and female) that caused him endless complications. What with the mess and the quarrelling at Cassino, Clark could not be but in agreement on this point: "I commanded also English, French, New Zealand and Indian troops; and I began to understand Napoleon when he said that it is better to fight against alliances rather than join them".

More attention needs to be given to the episode in which Lucas inadvertently clashed with Penney's susceptibilities. The story is told by Trevelyan, who mentions an euphoric bulletin from the Germans dated 7-8 February, at the outset of the counter-attack towards Aprilia, in which they boasted of having taken eight hundred prisoners in one swift blow: Scots Guards, Irish Guards and part of a battalion of the Staffordshire. It was a blow which caused Lucas to write: "I wish I had an American division in there. It is probably my fault that I don't understand them better. They are certainly brave men but our are better trained in my opinion, and I am sure that our officers are better educated in a military way". "Unfortunately", conclude Trevelyan, "he did not conceal these opinions. It was not surprising the General Penney 'seemed rather irritated' ".

Since this was the way things were, no-one can free Lucas from a certain element of bias. Any good trainer knows that if there is no solidarity in the team, if the weakest player is not encouraged, if they don't all help one another are preparing to defeat, not victory. But Lucas wrote down his criticisms day by day during the month that he was in Nettuno-Anzio, recording them in that intimate strong-box which every personal diary provides. From this diary, deposited in the military archives of Carlisle Barracks in Pennsylvania, Trevelyan was able to deduce all that was going on in the mind and heart of the American commander. However, how did it also get around by word of mouth? With whom did Lucas confide? Who was the gossip who let Penney in on his thoughts?

In such a well-documented work as that of the English writer, rich in first-hand interviews, some kind of affirmation similarly documented would surely not have been out of place even on this apparently secondary matter, all the more so because Penney, the person least likely to keep quiet about Lucas' shortcoming, never accused him of lack of discretion, reserve of tact. It should be also mentioned Penney' *Dispatch*, written after the war, quoted by the historian Carlo D'Este (*Fatal Decision*, p. 7): "...as many of those critical of Lucas's leadership at Anzio nevertheless fully supported his decision not to advance on Rome or to the Alban Hills immediately after the Shingle landings. They include his strongest critic, the commander of the 1st British Division, Major General W.R.C. Penney, who scoffed at the notion. 'We could have had one night in Rome and 18 months in P.W. camps".

At that time the General Penney (born in Edinburgh in 1896 and died in 1964) had retired to his home in the Berkshire countryside. After the surrender of Germany, he had had to go off to the war with Japan in the wake of Lord Louis Mountbatten, the maternal uncle of the Duke of Edinburgh. With Mountbatten, Commander-in-Chief of the British forces in South-East Asia and then Viceroy of India until the proclamation of independence in August 1947 and for a few months, Governor-General in Dehli, Penney took on the post of head of the information service. His battlefield was now a desk. At the beach-head on 18th February, a piece of shrapnel had injured him in the neck. He also suffered from a kidney complaint, and had been operated. He ended his career in London, in a office of the Admiralty, and gradually came to enjoy just strolling down the Mall.

He came back to our part of the world in 1952, after Alexander and Queen Elizabeth, to visit the British War Cemetery at Falasche. Visits from his family were more frequent, and indeed they were even planted a branch right in the town of Nettuno. His niece Anne, a daughter of his elder brother Joseph, married to the Italian engineer Sidney Prima Ricotti and has been living since 1964 in an apartment in the baronial building between Piazza Colonna and St. Giovanni's church. Of the General's own daughter, Sarah and Mary, the latter has often taken advantage of her husband visits to Rome, as an official of the Bank of England, to stay for a while with Anne and see the place where her father fought.

-So what did Penney have to say within the family about the landing, and about his dispute with Lucas?

"I ought to say first of all", his niece replies, "that my uncle and I met very rarely. He was always roaming about the world, even in peacetime, because of his army commitments. I was born in Alexandria, in Egypt, where my father was working with the British Embassy in Cairo. I went to school in England, but after I married I hardly

ever saw any more of my grandparents' home in Scotland".
-You must have gathered something from your cousin, though?
"Oh, yes. I'm very close to them. I have to go to Rome every day for my work with Cidim (an Italian musical organization, that works under the auspice of UNESCO). As soon as I get back to Nettuno, one of the things I like doing best is phoning Mary or Sarah. Undoubtedly Mary, who was closest to him, knows everything, however, that she could learn from magazine and books, because her father never said anything about himself relating to military matters".
-What about when Lucas attacked him in his diary?
"Not even then. My uncle was very reserved. Because of the position of responsibility ha had held, he believed that all his experiences were top secret. Only when he retired did he allow anything personal to come out. Mary knows how much Vaughan-Thomas had to beg him: in the end the general couldn't say no to the war correspondent who had been beside him in those difficult moments".
From Penney's notebooks or from his unpublished diary Vaughan-Thomas managed to extrapolate something of importance to put into his own book.

This was the dispatch with which the Scotsman informed Lucas, while German pressure was growing, that his troops could no longer defend Aprilia and Carroceto: "The 1st Division needs help". He also used a passage from the letter the general had left bound to write on the 10th of February after the fall of Aprilia, again to the commander of 6th Corps, giving him all particulars about the weakened state of his division: "...sapped by a desperate defense, and by constant contact with the enemy... a period of rest, refitting and reorganization is essential. The process of relief has started, but effective stabilization can, in my opinion, only be achieved by a strong counter-offensive... nothing in the above is to be interpreted as critical or defeatist...".
The "process of relief" refers to the fact that Lucas had already sent an armored detachment and an artillery and infantry unit of the American 45th Division to the aid of the sector which was in crisis. Moreover, it had been decided to launch a counter-attack. Lucas' Chief-of-Staff had telephoned to Penney that he same 45th Division would have to retake Aprilia. But the Americans, who broke out at 6:30 a.m. on 11th February, found themselves on the morning after, at the same point from where they had set out, partly because the bad weather, with heavy showers and gusts of wind for three

days in succession, had deprived them of air support.

As far as the English were concerned, Lucas was again to blame: "This counter-attack went the way of all the others that the Allies had launched; once again it was too weak and too late. General Lucas was still unwilling to commit his reserves, for he knew that the storm now breaking over his lines had not yet reached its full fury. His theme was, in Vaughan-Thomas diagnosis: "There's worse to come. He was determinate to hoard his reserves to the last". When he had seen the files of both parties concerned, he could also envisage what it was that compromised the unity of the Allies: "It would be idle to pretend that at this stage of the battle Penney had confidence in the vigor of Corps leadership or that Lucas felt sure of the British capacity to hold. So the arguments raged behind the lines...".

Meanwhile, the Germans, having assembled at Aprilia and Carroceto and itching to attack, could prepare themselves for the assault ordered by Hitler: "The beach-head", so ran his message, "is an abscess which must be lanced with urgency". By order of Kesserling, the command of the 14th Army had left Verona for the south, and hence the whole area around Rome was entrusted to General Eberhard von Mackensen. This general and

Kesserling, who was keeping the whole front under his supervision, flying over every morning from mount Soratte, where the German headquarters had been transferred after Frascati had been devastated by the air bombardment of the 8th September, had planned 'Operation Fishfang' for 16th February: an assault which was meant to feed the Anglo-American to the fish.

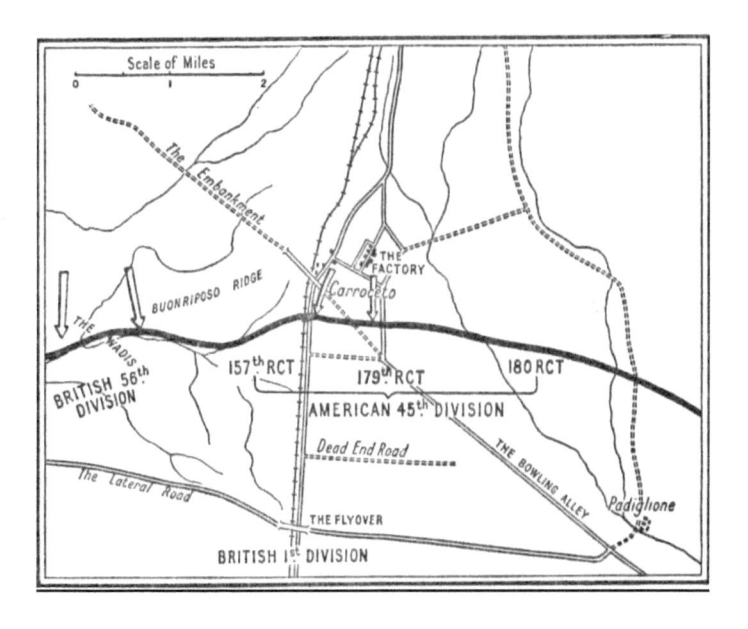

The beginning of the final German assault, took place on 16th February, 1944 which according to Hitler, who was directing it from Germany, should have thrown the Allies back into the sea.

ANZIO-NETTUNO BEACH HEAD

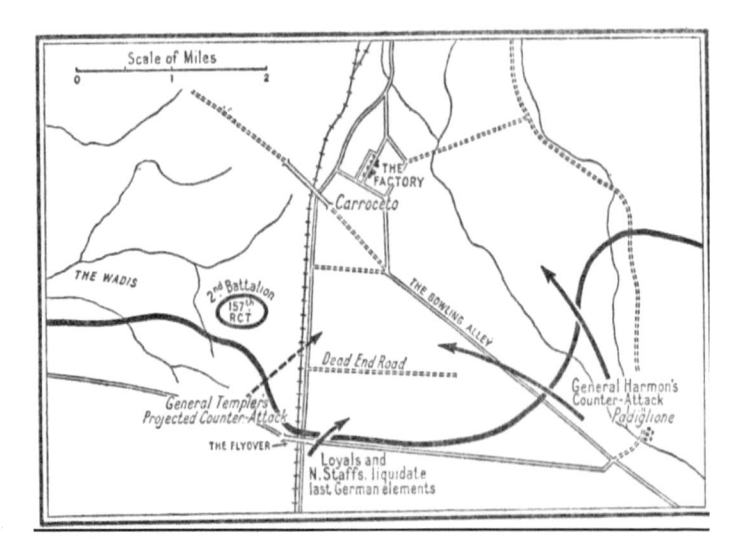

On February 19th the Allies were on the verge of disaster, but nevertheless reacted in such a way that the Germans, now being subjected to massive aerial bombardments, was halted definitively. Hitler demanded that Kesserling and Mackensen make another attempt to break through on the Cisterna side, but that was soon quashed by the Americans.

ANZIO-NETTUNO BEACH HEAD

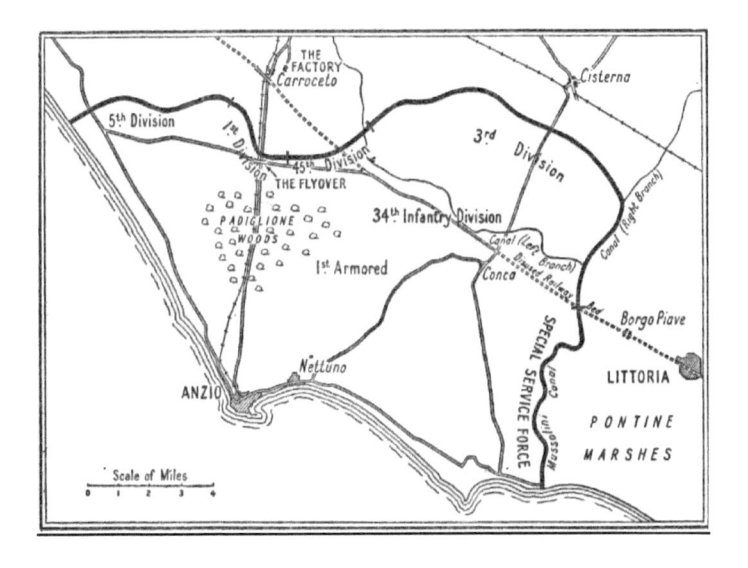

By March 1st, 1944 the German forces were exhausted. From then on, the armies remained facing one another.

ANZIO-NETTUNO BEACH HEAD

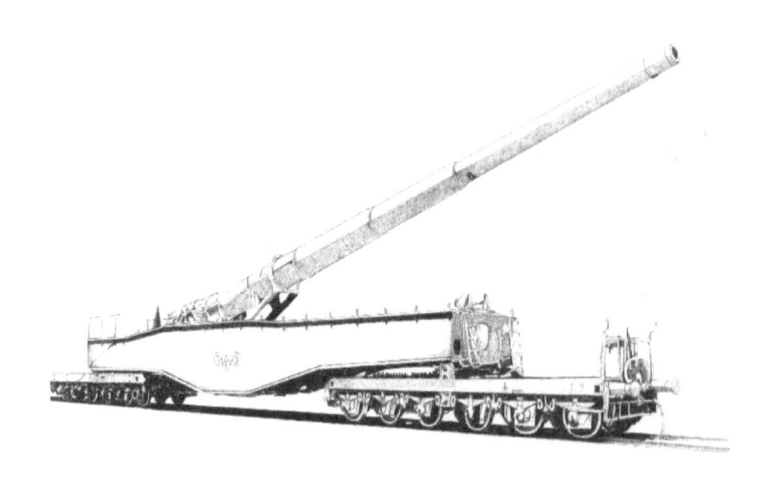

In addition to air raids it must be taken into account the firing from the two big railway guns 'Leopold' and 'Robert'. The drawing indicates its size and features. Designed by Krupp, under the abbreviation 28 cm K 5 (E), the guns had a body measuring 21.538 meters, with a range up to 38 miles, and weighed a total of 218 tons. The Germans had the two guns at their disposal against the beachhead. They were kept hidden in the Villa Senni tunnel in Frascati and brought out to shoot at Ciampino Station.

THE GUNS IN THE TUNNEL

In the meantime German propaganda was broadcasting a continuous, throbbing slogan over Radio Rome: "Beach-head = Death-head". Bur everything was throbbing at Nettuno-Anzio, beginning with the two big guns which were mounted on railway wagons and peered out of the Rome-Frascati tunnel. They fired, then retreated into their lairs, foiling the fighter bombers which flew vainly overhead, trying to knock them out. Named 'Leopold' by the Germans and nicknamed 'Anzio Annie' or 'Anzio Express' by the Allies, even when it was thought that there was only one piece of artillery, they were monsters. They required the assistance of ten attendants and with each explosion, in our case the explosion required to fire 255 kg. shell up to 30 miles, they sent an earth tremor over the whole surrounding countryside.

Their psychological effect can be compared with that of the Flying Bombs and the fist missiles, the V2's, which terrorized London during Hitler's last months and, with their whistle and crash at all hours of the day and night, claimed almost ten thousand victims. Those who were subjected to 'Annie' and 'Express' suffered the same shock: "First you heard a distant, almost discreet cough,

ANZIO-NETTUNO BEACH HEAD

away behind the enemy lines, then a slight pause, during which you knew the shell was on its way. Fear wound up your guts... then came the sickening crump of the explosion and the sound echoed away like a tube train pulling out of the station... maybe the shell did not do much great material damage, but there was no question that it damages nerves and morale". (Vaughan-Thomas, *Op. cit.* pp. 132-133).

Major Tompinks, the extremely active service agent of the Fifth Army, was certainly the most informed about goings-on in Italian circles. Even Benedetto Croce mentions him. In his diary of "When Italy was divided in two" the visit he made to Capri on 22nd September 1943, together with General Donovan and the journalist Whitaker, with the aim of organizing an insurrection of the people of Naples against the Germans. Both Clark and Truscott, having tried with the then inadequate radar, to retrace the cannon-fire back to its starting point, asked him to discover the hiding-place of these two moveable railway-borne cannons. Tompkins located them. But the Allies planes never had time in a nose-dive to nab them: and one suspects they didn't even try, perhaps because they didn't put much faith in the spy in Rome, to silence them with a sustained bombardment that would have blocked the entrance and the exit to the tunnel.

The diverging opinions among the war correspondents only increase this suspicion. They were all convinced that they had put their finger on the point from where the cannons fired, here, here, but they all indicated different places: Marino, Castelgandolfo, Albano, Lanuvio, Cecchina, Campoleone. Vaughan-Thomas, in his book published eighteen years after the landing, continued to shroud the matter in mystery: "Who knows where they were hidden". They were hidden, one behind the other, on the same track and inside the same tunnel: the old Villa Senni tunnel which had been the pride of Pope Pius IX when the first railway line belonging to the Pontifical State, the Rome-Frascati line, was inaugurated on 7th July, 1865.

The entrance to this gallery is three kilometers beyond Ciampino. Regularly every evening, or in the morning on rainy days, the two 'super guns' came out and went into action at Ciampino Station, where the numerous tracks enabled the cannons to be maneuvered. Remo Tempesta, an elderly railwayman who was resident in Ciampino, saw them in action from his window: "They were right there under my eyes, because I used to live above the railway line, at the tower of Acqua Sotterra, halfway between the station and the tunnel. One at a time, they would each shoot six shots, at intervals of a few minutes. Often they would disappear in a furious hurry after one or two shots, because Allies planes had been seen. They were frightening especially at night, when their cannon-fire flashed like a red-hot ball".

This account is backed up by research carried out by Raimondo Del Nero, Professor of Italian and History at the E. Fermi Institute of Frascati. He got his clue from one of the school's janitors, Giuseppe Martinelli. He, too, had witnessed all the commotion inside the Villa Senni tunnel in 1944. Professor Del Nero, who writes for the magazine 'Castelli Romani' whose editor, Nello Nobiloni, like an archeologist continue to 'dig' among the stones and traditions of Frascati and the surrounding districts. The article he published in July-August 1985 was an invitation to climb the 'Maschio of Lariano' (891 meters), in the Artemisio chain, behind Velletri.

He wrote, amongst other things: 'The strategic importance of the Maschio of Lariano' was rediscovered in 1944, after the Allied landing at Anzio. The Germans installed there an observation post, the walls of which are still recognizable. This directed the artillery's shelling of the beach-head and, in particular, gave the firing instructions to the two railway guns hidden in the tunnel, in the vicinity of Frascati.

Further, albeit indirect confirmation, came from the reminiscences collected by Andrea Caracci, president of the Marino Tourist Office: from Mario Fabrizi, stationmaster of Campoleone and Ciampino, then retired in Marino; and from Paolo Emili, president of the 'Castrum Candulfi', an association set up to safeguard the treasures of Castelgandolfo. Having eliminated the possibilities of Campoleone, Cecchina and Lanuvio, all these accounts esclude that even one single gun could hide in the tunnel of the De Paolis hill, two kilometers from Marino, or in that of the Ferentano woods, just outside Marino, or in the Barberini Villa tunnel outside the Castelgandolfo Station, at the level-crossing on the bank of the lake, or in that of Villa Doria, just inside Albano. They exclude it because since the aerial bombing of Marino on 2nd February, right up until the American's arrival, evacuee were living in the tunnels.

It is also known exactly where and how 'Annie' and 'Express' ended up. (Their names actually were Leopold and Robert). According to Trevelyan, 'Annie' was found in a tunnel at Nemi. (It is here that the fleeing Germans had set fire to the museum of Caligola's two ships, both of which were destroyed.) It could be that towards the end at least one of the guns had been moved. It is not likely, however, that the tunnel was just a stone's through from the 'strawberry town', which was not then, and is not now, on the railway line. But was this actually 'Annie' or was it 'Express'?

When the Gustav line was destroyed in May, and Cassino taken, and when the link-up with the army of Nettuno-Anzio was made, and the advance towards Rome begun, the Allies forced the enemy to retreat without one of the big guns, which was sabotaged before being abandoned. It must have been the one Trevelyan mentions. The other one ended up later in the hands of the Americans, who seized it intact in June at the Civitavecchia railway station. Clark had the main pieces of the first collected together and, along with the second, they crossed the ocean on a Liberty. A model has been reconstructed in the USA from 'Express' and the remains of 'Annie' or vice versa, and this, named Leopold, is now in Virginia at Fort Lee, where it was moved recently from Aberdeen in Maryland. And after it was studied carefully and tried out, it was put on show for the public.

As a warning to all, there should be a permanent exhibition of the consequences of war. But, on the contrary, the powers that be often hide their excesses behind the protective screen of state security, and thus decide what the public should or should not know. Even in the best established democracies, well immunized against the disease of censorship, one of the most frequent debates concerns the freedom of the press: is it right to publish everything, or there should be some sort of corrective?

The temptation to impose the latter must be strong, if even some of the high executor of law and justice are not immune from it. This we saw in Italy in the case of some journalists arrested for giving away official secrets. So what would the President, the Congress and the Supreme Court of United States have felt compelled to do with the anti-Roosevelt editor of the newspaper 'Tribune' of Chicago, who gave away the new that the Americans knew the Japanese secret code, thus inviting them immediately to invent another? Send him to the Electric Chair? Or should there be recourse to a special law, which renders all information of national concern taboo?

On Bedloe Island, the Statue of Liberty has never had cause to blush over such provisions. The American Press, even in less glorious moments such as the denunciation of massacre in Vietnam, and the Watergate affair which caused Nixon to throw in the sponge, has shown that the people who are really free are those who know the truth.

But in Nettuno-Anzio, in the days of the crisis, the truth was very unpleasant, and the Allied Command did not want everyone to know it. Apart from not communicating any further news to the journalists who appeared every morning at the cellar in Via Romana occupied by Joe Langevin, the head of the Press Office, it withdrew all permits to send reports from the beach-head. The result was that they sowed panic among the nation's editorial offices, which were bubbling with the most disparate rumors from Naples and Algiers.

The black-out explained the generals in the field, had been provoked by the actual newspaper headlines coming from Naples, which had appeared at the front. How can one obtain sacrifices from one's own soldiers when they are being discouraged by what they read? The ideal for them would have been that "the correspondents ceased writing until the danger had passed, or if their writing were subject to a far stricter scrutiny... everything would have been so much simpler if the war-correspondents had remained safely back at Caserta and Naples writing up the war from the handouts at Army headquarters". (Vaughan-Thomas, *Op. cit.* p. 144).

It was Alexander who, on 14th February, brought the correspondents together in Nettuno and took them to task. Certainly, he didn't accuse them of being collaborators of the Germans, but nor did he say that they were collaborators of the Allied Army, considering what they dictated to their papers. He rejected their protests with a question: "Where any of you at Dunkirk?". Nobody answered. "I was", he said, "and I know that there's never likely to be a Dunkirk here". However, Lucas was not sufficiently reassured, and he confided to his diary: "The correspondents were furious. I had to come to terms for the first time with the fact that people could seriously think of our defeat... I felt a nasty spasm of fear".

From the correspondent point of view, there were broader consideration. About twenty years later, seeing things in a more detached light, Vaughan-Thomas drew a reassuring moral from the affair: "Alexander, a reasonable man, felt the strength of the protests, and promised that the whole thing should be checked when he returned to Naples... could you have imagined it taking place at Kesserling's headquarters, or behind the front of the Red Army? The Commander-in-Chief took time in a crisis of the battle to meet the correspondents and he struggled to see the viewpoint of the press... it was a part of the democracy that the Allies were trying to defend".

Such defense, of course, has to be total. If we do not take into account the conflict between freedom of the press and power, we risk playing up to those who are interested in avoiding the issue. Take Churchill, for instance, he believed that the broadcasts of the American NBC news network were 'catastrophic', as were the reports of the London 'Evening Standard', the 'Daily Mail' and others papers, which at that point could not overlook that on the Anzio-Nettuno front the initiative had passed to the enemy. He was more disturbed than Alexander, while Roosevelt admitted that the situation was tense. "Why all the defeatism?", Churchill asked, "the censorship should have been imposed to stop the circulation of these alarmist rumors". (Trevelyan, *Op,cit.* p. 159).

So said the prime Minister, as Prime Minister. But he too had once been a journalist. In October 1899, when he was twenty-five, he was sent by the 'Morning Post' to South Africa; for a fee of two hundred and fifty pounds and all expenses paid, he was to keep Her Britannic Majesty's subjects informed about the war with the Boers. His reports were based on what he saw, and not on what the High Command passed on (later, he made his opinion of the Commander of the expedition, General Redvers Buller, much clearer when he wrote that he "was capable of going from one stupidity to another, from disaster to disaster,

without losing his popularity either with the British people or with his troops").
What, then could Churchill the journalists expect with these reports? "The unpleasant truths which I wrote about", so he summed things up, "raised a lot of indignation. My statement that 'the Boer who is firing individually, moving about on horseback in familiar terrain, is worth from three to five regulars' was taken as an insult to our soldiers. My claim that it was necessary to put a quarter of a million men into the line was dismissed as absurd... the old colonels and generals of the Buck and Dodder Club were beside themselves: some of them sent me a telegram saying: 'Your faithful friends in this Club hope you will stop making a fool of yourself'. But in fact events soon proved my foolish words right. Ten thousand men were sent to reinforce our effective strength in South Africa, among them those of the Imperial Yeomanry and other formations. And, before we finally gained the victory, they were joined on South African soil by a quarter of a million English soldiers. They had taken me for a child, but I was able to console myself with the Biblical saying: Better a child that is poor and wise than a king that is a fool". (Churchill, *My Early Living*, p. 312-313).
A first-rate journalist, then. His own experiences, however, and the fundamental role of a free and

ANZIO-NETTUNO BEACH HEAD

vigilant press, slipped his memory, and other journalists faithfully reported the unpleasant truths about Anzio-Nettuno, as he himself had reported the unpleasant truths about South Africa. This does not means that he closed his eyes to reality. This was described by the correspondents on who, he had imposed silence, and Churchill was well aware of it. "The expected major effort to drive us back into the sea opened on February 16th, when the enemy employed, from Campoleone to south, over four divisions, supported by 450 guns... the attack fell at an awkward moment, as American reinforcements and the 56th British Division, transferred from the Cassino front, were just relieving out gallant 1st Division, who soon found themselves in full action again. A deep, dangerous wedge was driven into our line, which was forced back here to the beach-head... all hung in the balance. No further retreat was possible... I had no illusions about the issue. It was life or death". (Churchill, *Op, cit.*, p.433).

KESSERLING WAS CERTAIN

Kesserling was already tasting victory. He had put aside the idea of beginning the attack from along the coast, with the paratroops of the 4th Division, concentrated at Ardea: then pushing along the road to Tor S. Lorenzo and Lido dei Pini. The plan would have allowed the Germans to take the Allied line-up on its flank, but would have exposed his troops to bombardment from the sea by the Allied ships. For this reason he decided on the frontal attack, face to face, on the road to Campoleone (which is the Nettunense), as Churchil records. From the outposts in Aprilia and Carroceto, already conquered, it seemed to Kesserling that he had a push-over: "I myself was convinced, even taking their powerful naval guns and overwhelming air superiority into consideration, that with the means available we must succeed in throwing the Allies back into the sea. I was trying to assess the American 6th Corps' capacity to resist, also from the psychological point of view; and by then their conditions must have been insupportable". (Kesserling, *A Soldier's story*, p. 214).

It has been estimated that at that point 100.000 Allied soldiers were surrounded by about 125.000

Germans. Among these was also an Italian contingent, whom it would be unfair to dismiss in bulk as fascists. Indeed not all of them were, and a good many who signed up in the 'Decima Mas' had only followed the example of their commander, another Borghese Prince. Junio Valerio. He was a frigate commander and submariner, gold-medal, who on the 8th September refused to sail from La Spezia with the fleet which, following Badoglio's order and the Armistice clauses, was headed for Malta to turn itself over to the Allies.

Most of them were students grown up in system which had eliminated the word democracy from the textbooks. They were nurtured not on ideal of freedom, but rather on concepts of exaltation, the Superman, Boldness, D'Annunzio Lyricism, Giovanni Gentile's Actualism, the Roman Empire. As a result, these boys came to believe that the choice was between betrayal and military honor, and that one could not but be on the Germans' side, especially in the face of defeat. Trapped in the constrictions of a short-sighted culture, which was a sort of drug, they ignored that without freedom it is impossible to have peace, social justice and a secure country. They did not know that there were men like Sandro Pertini opposed to the 'Decima Mas', which came under the authority of Karl

Wolff, head of the SS in Italy, and was used against the partisans.

No-one had ever told them about all this. It took the liberation of Italy to discover that, in the years of oceanic crowd gathering, an Italian, who had been condemned by Fascism to prison and exile, and who suffered from tuberculosis, had written to his mother: "I consider you dead", just because she had asked Mussolini to pardon him. When Enzo Biagi interviewed Pertini at Montecitorio in 1974, he explained: "That was a cruel letter for my mother, but I would have contradicted my principles had I submitted to the dictatorship". The journalist was moved: "For the first time, an interview ended in an embrace. It never happened to me before".

The Germans admitted only one battalion from the Decima Mas, the 'Barbarigo', to the Nettuno-Anzio front, one month after the landing. It fought at Cisterna and Campoverde, and along the Moscarello Canal. Another unit, made up of artillerymen from the 'St. Giorgio group', went into action at Sermoneta and Bassiano. The 'Degli Oddi Battalion' as part of the Italian SS, arrived almost at the same time as the 'Barbarigo'. Before them, a few paratrooper platoon from the 'Nembo' and one regiment of the 'Folgore' had been incorporated into the forces facing the British at the Moletta Ditch near Aprilia.

However, the sailors from the 'Decima Mas' were present in Nettuno-Anzio already by mid-September and October, following the German Occupation. They were a Garrison patrol who came and went from the Villa Borghese by order of their commander Valerio, cousin of Rodolfo, the father of Don Steno. The latter was afraid that the German Colonel Scholl (who had put down the resistance of the Anzio and Nettuno people, took the command and then handed over to Lt. Querbach) might confiscate the villa. So, he asked for his uncle's assistance. The tiny detachment from the 'Decima Mas' left Nettuno-Anzio as soon as Borghese were sure of their immunity being guaranteed by the Germans.

This, more than the fact that he had upheld the local administration after the 8th September, made Don Steno a dangerous element for the Allied information service, and they included him in its list of enemies. The Americans ordered his arrest and this was carried out on the morning of the landing, as we know, by a young Colonel William Darby, one of the West Point's most brilliant pupils, who commanded the Rangers. But they realized in a short time that the Prince was really a friend, and, offering him their apologies, begged him to continue to serve as mayor of Anzio-Nettuno. Their collaboration increased during the height of the German attack. Don Steno covered his head with the helmet that had protected his father during the First World War, and considering himself a fully-fledged front-line fighter, to such an extent that he willingly opened up his villa to the Fifth Army advanced headquarters.

The events that followed would show that Valerio and Don Steno, although lined up on opposite fronts, were not so different in their desire to protect their properties. The 'Decima Mas' commander was not unprepared when in April 1945, time came for the rendering of accounts. As he had access to channels through which to contact the Allies and negotiate his capitulation, he managed to elude the partisans who intended to hang him from the petrol pump in Piazzale Loreto. Two agents of the Office of Strategic Service rushed to take him in Milan, giving him only the time to put on the uniform of an American Lieutenant and then took him in their jeep to the more salubrious air of Rome.

His nephew was accustomed to this type of painless solution. He returned his uncle's favor from the other side of the barricade, recommendding him in due time to Clark. Junio Valerio died in Spain in 1974. Don Steno four years later in Rome. They are both buried on the same shelf, in the crypt of the Basilica of St. Maria Maggiore in Rome.

We had left Field-Marshall Kesserling in the middle of the penalty area, on the verge of scoring a goal, with Eberhard von Mackensen by his side. But the strings of the entire operation were pulled by Hitler in his favorite residence of Berchtesgaden in upper Bavaria. Hailed by official propaganda as 'the greatest Napoleon of all times', he didn't give a moment's respite to any of his generals. Erwin Rommel knew something about this. The 'Wustenfuchs', the 'Desert Fox', the brilliant commander of the Afrika Corps, had fallen into disgrace for having proposed in November '43 a strategic withdraw from north of Rome, following that of El Alamein. "I am tired of withdrawing generals", Hitler told him, and immediately decided to hand over to Kesserling the command of the armies in Italy.

Neither did the lance-corporal hesitate to impart his lesson to the helmsmen.

After the sinking of the 'Bismark', the Great-Admiral Erich Raecher, chief of the Navy before Karl Dönitz, felt his hands tied by rulings which required any action by large units in the Atlantic to be submitted first for Hitler's approval. No wonder then that at Nettuno-Anzio it was always he who gave the orders. Not only did he insist that the privilege of delivering the first punch fell on the infantry regiment of Lehr, a group of select Nazis sent from Germany. He also modified the plan of Kesserling and von Mackensen, who would have preferred to move inland spreading themselves cut at the same time to avoid the concentration in one spot of the Allied artillery and air raids.

Hitler did not allow this: the German 14th Army had to deal its blow towards the sea, without dispersing itself on peripheral targets. Even the Lehr Infantry, all of them young men trained to the shout of "Hiel Hitler", but with no knowledge of the ground they were about to penetrate, imposed on Kesserling yet another route reversal. He usually attacked in the dark of the night and in bad weather, which ensured him the absence of the American Air Force. This time, the bulk of the German offensive set off at dawn, so as to allow the newcomers to see where they were going.

This strategy didn't suffice to save them. There was a bit of a skirmish on the Cisterna front, which was meant to serve as a diversion. The young Nazis crouched behind the Panzers made their move at 6:30 a.m. east of Aprilia, advancing until they came under fire and were dispersed at midday. Kesserling judged their behavior to be ignominious, and waited until night-time to charge once more suitable men. The Allied defense was overwhelmed from a point on the Nettunense highway, inland as far as the fly-over bridge at Campo di Carne, and as far as across as the Padiglione tower. Hence, the wedge to which Churchill referred had been opened. On the morning of the 17th February, while newly appointed deputy commander Truscott was consigning the 3rd Division to O'Daniel and Darby, and in the headquarters of Via Romana they were insistently asking about him, General Laurence B. Keiser, Chief of General Staff, observed: "He had better hurry, because I don't know whether tomorrow there will still be a headquarters".

The next day Clark arrived in his plane, a 'Piper Cub' escorted by 'Spitfires'. The shooting range airstrip had been bombed just after a Nettuno team working for the American Engineers has repaired it, so Clark had to land on an adjacent road. "What are your proposals", he asked Lucas and Truscott, "for holding off the Germans?". "We have to counter-attack with every means", replied Truscott. And Clark confirmed that the entire Mediterranean air-force would be there, with one raid after another, to back the German army.

The counter-attack which avoided another Dunkirk, took place north of the fly-over bridge at

Campo di Carne by a column leaded by General Gerald W.B. Templer, commander of the British 56th Infantry Division, on the outskirts of the Padiglione woods, beyond Campoverde with General Harmon's tanks; it achieved its purpose. The Germans lost the battle on a strip of land cleared for the Pontina highway which the Allies had marked on their maps as 'Bowling Alley'. On 19th February, on this leveled ground, definitely more appropriate for 'bowling', the American tanks fired non-stop from 6 a.m. to 4:20 p.m.

The firing was witnessed by a Calabrian schoolboy, Ernesto Astorino, son of the Nettuno tax collector. Ernesto was a high-school student about to get his degree in classical studies. After the 8th September he had stopped commuting to Rome, to attend the Giosuè Carducci High School. His family had evacuated to the farmhouse of Paolo Bragalone, a farmer with one of the largest estates in Campo di Bove: around 20 hectares, on the border of the Campana. Ernesto was among the first to offer his services to the Americans and they employed him with the 36th group of Engineers. He was paid only a handful of Am-lire, but the job earned him several tins of food to soothe his raging hunger: it consisted in collecting the plaster debris from the mountains of rubble from the bombed houses, with the help of bulldozers. The debris was used in the countryside, especially on marshlands, to facilitate the transit of carts. Another endless task needing Ernesto's assistance was that of digging trenches.

From one of these trenches, not more than 500 meters away, Ernesto saw the Sherman tanks in operation: "Before they could advance, at least one hundred of them formed a semi-circle, shooting one shell after another against the mass of Germans. For hours on end, the mouths of the tanks were spitting flames. Finally, one could see, through the smoke, the blurred outline of the enemy turning back. They then started coming forward groups through the burning Panzers with their hands up. To the side of me, more tank Shermans were crossing the Carroceto road. The sun was setting, and then I noticed, hanging out of the turrets of a vast number of tanks red-hot cannon barrels, bent and nearly molten from the heat of repeated fire".

Hitler, 'willpower personified', as Churchill defined him on that occasion, did not give up. Rather than guessing, he took for granted that the landing corps was on the verge of collapse, bled and exhausted as it was. He thus ordered Kesserling and von Mackensen to gather their forces and shift the attack to the American flank, from Cisterna towards Nettuno. Kesserling knew he had spent all his resources and that it was the Germans and not the Americans who were bleeding. But how to explain this to the lance-corporal who insistently shouted "Attack! Attack!". The German 14th Army, put under pressure, managed nevertheless to get a few days for preparation, during which it tried to mask its intentions. All kinds of tricks were continuously devised on all fronts. At the Teheran Conference, Stalin had delighted in showing Churchill how the Red Army had always duped the Germans in its offensives, amassing elsewhere papier-mâché tanks and airplanes. The Americans, whose industry was in the forefront in all areas, including that of rubber and plastics, devised something that evoked one of child's greatest enchantments, those colored balloons on a string that take life's first dreams with them when they escape from childish clutches and disappear into the sky- Anything but balloons were the air containers blown up to the shape and size of Sherman tanks and placed at night a long way from the munitions depots, which made their appearance with the light of day to trick the German artillery.

With another means, that is with the forces labor of various Roman carpenters, especially film- set builders from Cinecittà, Kesserling constructed groups of false Panzers and cannons around

Genzano, Albano and Ardea, thus giving the idea of another attack on the British positions. But they were warned by Tompkins. The last German attempt originated from Cisterna on 29th February. They were aided by downpours of rain that held back the airplanes. It didn't get far and only lasted a short time. After having made some progress at Carano, where they defeated a company of parachutists from the 509th Battalion, the Wehrmacht was forced to retrace its steps.

"On March 1st Kesserling accepted his failure. He had frustrated the Anzio expedition. He could not destroy the beach-head". Thus wrote Churchill congratulating himself with Roosevelt for the danger escaped and, in particular, for the heroism of the US 3rd Division. Kesserling took it sportingly enough: "In general the enemy had twice as many divisions as we had. In this battle, however, the Germans had more. But even when we have taken into account our own weakness in action, as well as the Allies aerial superiority and their naval back-up, I must say that it was the combined American 6th Corps, with the magnificent show they put on, who repulsed us". (Kesserling, *Op. cit.*, p. 216).

For Hitler, this represented the beginning of the end. He reacted with a fit of anger, summoning about 20 officers and soldiers from the Italian front to help him find out who was responsible for the failure of 'Operation Fishfang'. This witnesses, flown on 4th March to Berchtesgaden, had to withstand two days' interrogation. General Walther Fries stood his ground and Hitler was placated. It had been neither a betrayal nor an act of negligence. It had been the superior numbers of the Allied cannons, tanks, ships and, above all, airplanes. They were outnumbered 300 to 4000, or even 6000.

This coincided with what General Westphal had personally explained to him on Kesserling's behalf. He was received for the last time on 6th March, when it took him three hours to convince him Hitler of the truth which was gripping at Germany's throat: "Just as I was about to take leave from him, he showed signs of being moved. He said he realized the extent of the exhaustion of the German people and the Wehrmacht, and that he was ready to seek a quick solution. To this end, he added, what was needed was a victory".

A victory that would have been supportive of a negotiation with the Allies, with the aim of avoiding unconditional surrender. It was the Führer's last illusion: which accompanied him to the basement of the Berlin Chancery where, clutching Eva Braun, he committed suicide with her. It was 30th April 1945 and, two blocks away, the Russians were advancing. Hitler thought it appropriate to point out in him memorial: "My wife and I would rather die than face the disgrace of defeat".

TONY'S WAR

Tony was out in the open air the morning of the landing. He was eighteen years old and already had a few months military experience, having managed to enlist in the Navy as a volunteer. His full name is Antonio Taurelli, and was renamed Tony by the Americans. His return from Pola, in the confusion of the 8th September, was an odyssey. It ended up in wooden hut on his family's vineyard at Seccia area, where they all lived on top of another: his mother Tommasina, his sisters Egle and Marisa and his aunt Angelina with her five children.

He ran into the Americans at the Martufi dairy farm, just as dawn was breaking. He had gone to get some milk, and the Americans were heating up some coffee. What a relief for Tony to hear them speaking Italian, a mixture of Abruzzo and Neapolitan dialects! But the voice, several hours later, which had the effect of enticing him to join the US Army, was that of an officer with Spanish origins: Lt. Stanley R. Navas, who was marching at the head of a company of paratroopers from the 504th Regiment, the same one that Churchill wanted drop behind the German lines.

Instead, they had to go slowly on foot, struggling up from the beach after midday. It was on the wide and unsurfaced Frati road, that Navas saw Tony. He called to him: "Where are the Germans? Tony, with his cousin Rolando, approached the lieutenant: "Down there, at Le Ferriere", and then proceeded to follow him.

The paratroopers followed a different itinerary. On their maps, there was an arrow leading to a bridge, marked Number 2, on the Moscarello Canal. The boy offered himself as a guide: "Take me with you". Navas eyed him from head to foot: "Okay", but as for Rolando, he shook his head: "He's too young. Send him home".

"From then up to 11th April, when the 504th sailed from Naples for England", tells us Tony, "I was one of those paratroopers, and as for the battle to defend Nettuno against the Germans returning, I fed it all".

-Armed and in uniform like them?

"We spent the night in the scrub of St. Antonio, to the left of the new farmhouse, on the Gnif Gnaf district's road. In the morning, as he handed me over to lance-corporal Branch, Lt. Navas told him what had been decided: that I had been enrolled in the 504th Regiment. I received a uniform, a rifle and the task of loading the machine-gun".

-Where did you shoot?

ANZIO-NETTUNO BEACH HEAD

"Our war with the Germans started and ended around Borgo Podgora, between the Moscarello Canal and Pantano ditch, in the slime of the muddy, black pits, like the one by the 'Smerdino' bridge. We were on our bellies, glued to the embankments, often caught between the enemy fire and that of the Allied artillery, and we saw nothing but dead and wounded".
-What happened when the Germans tried to break through on your side?
"Every moment was a bad one for us, with the enemy only 300-400 meters away, on the other side of the canal which at that time was known as Mussolini Canal. One night, before Kesserling's last offensive, Lt. Navas himself waded across the canal with about 30 men. At the top of the embankment they were thrown back by the mines. We went to pull them out. Navas' left arm had been sheared off and his face was disfigured by the mine splinters. Lt. Richard W. Swenson substituted him. Of that German attack, the night, we never stopped shooting, a night full of blinding flashes, I still recall the desolation that filled me with the first light of day, when my eyes started to close. The woods, which had served as a curtain between us and the enemy, was no longer there; the remains of the tree-trunks were smoldering like cigarette butts".

ANZIO-NETTUNO BEACH HEAD

-Why was there a stalemate up to May?

"The 504th was recalled on 23rd March for the Overlord, and I left also. In the end, on the Pantano ditch, we had to watch out the German raids. There were some frightful scenes in the dark, one ambush after another, killing each other in silence, the paratroops with their daggers in their mouth and their faces blackened. The paratroopers had to take it in turn to go to a farmhouse in no-man's land, stay there 24 hours, and signal by telephone the night-time transit of the German patrols. This watch duty was indispensable if we didn't want to end up with our throats cut and I did it three times".

-Why were you left behind in Naples?

"Lt. Swenson and Sgt. Mark C. Williamson could not explain it to me. Like all paratroopers, I would rest at the Costanzo Ciano Barracks, in Bagnoli. On 11th April, the day of the departure for Liverpool, we got on a train headed to Naples, while my bag full of personal things, my rifle and my helmet were loaded on the lorries that were taking the regiment's luggage to the ship. Still, from Piazza Garibaldi to the port, no-one said anything to me. Under the gangway, lined up with the rest, I was stopped by Lt. Swenson: "Sorry, Tony, you can't come with us". He handed me a piece of paper with his signature, which attested that I had fought with the American Army against the Germans, in my own country. I had imagined quite a different sort of discharge".

This was the least of Tony's tragedy, Nettuno and Anzio, which had been crowded by the war, were once again empty. Far from the sea, mother earth who had opened her arms to her children, made homeless by the Germans, first lost her arms and then were totally mutilated. The peasants also, after all they had done to help the evacuees, were forced to leave. With his realism, or harshness and cynicism (depending on the extent of anti-militarist feeling), Lucas had immediately tackled the problem: "It's impossible to fight with women and children around".

What he meant, of course, was that it was necessary to take them away to safety. In the beginning, when even he could not foresee that events would drag out so long, he had advised the local population to stay inside the shelters and caves. The American hospital, equipped with operating rooms and rapidly set up in the Foglino woods, never turned down children or women. For that matter, it never sent back any of the Anzio-Nettuno people, although it had its hands more than full with the wounded and was itself damaged by the German bombs, as perhaps was inevitable in the general confusion. (On the other hand, the sinking of the hospital ship 'St. David' was avoidable and inexcusable, lit up as it was with Red Cross symbols.)

Italian doctors were given all possible support, so as to ensure medical assistance for the civilians. They were supplied with sanitary materials and whatever else they needed. Giovanni Cappella, a final-year medical student was useful adjunct. Evacuated with his family at La Ferriere district, he did not hesitate during the German occupation to put on a white coat and practice at the Latina hospital.

He went there every morning on his bicycle until the Americans assigned him a jeep, a driver and a helmet. His first operation, performed with instruments belonging to one of Nettuno's midwives 'Sora Bianca', was on 'Sora Bianca' herself. She had been wounded in the breast when a grenade exploded at Borgo Montello. Two years later, when Giovanni took his Degree, the midwife presented him with her instruments, still kept in their old wooden box.

But the drama of the war was centered at Anzio-Nettuno, and gave no sign of moving on. Besides, cohabitation with the local population became difficult for the Army, because of concurrences that aroused the Allies' suspicions, tormented as they were by the precision of the enemy's bombers.

How could they possibly manage to aim so well in the dark? It wasn't even necessary to aim or to use a sight, in view of the congestion in the area, it was enough to drop a bomb and something would blow up. However, the Military Police, maybe because it had a list of fascists and former fascists to keep an eye on, could see nothing but spies, intent on lighting up the Luftwaffe's target.

They immediately suspected the bakers, starting with those who had worked under the Germans. Margherita Ricci and her husband Romeo, were accused of collaborationism and locked up for 20 days, he in room of the Casa del Sole, she in the cave, and then sent to Naples. (Margherita, as a smart woman as she was, managed to get from the Allied Military Government, a suitcase full of rolls of Am-lire banknotes which she used to cut with big scissors. All of this money had been much of help to survive for her and for those who asked her for a loan, so did Nicola Catanzani's father, which could open a fruit and salad shop thanks to her help.) It was an American officer who took care of the bakers by sending them home: "You must not light up the oven again. The smoke could guide the German airplanes". And in front of Alfonso Bernardini's bakery, there too, were the Military Police ordering him to shut it down.

But is it possible to live without bread? When we look back at the past, some kind of yearning always returns. Perhaps it is the smell of the kneading-trough or the dirge of an ancient prayer: "...*our daily bread*...". In the diary in which Don Steno, from 15th January to the 10th June, recorded these sad events; there are two entries that would not be unworthy of the Book of Genesis: "29th January, about 26 quintals of grain and flour for the people to make their bread, found but not yet distributed; 4th February, arrival of first American flour for the population".

Together with the flour, the Nettuno-Anzio people also received bread and something to go with it. At least Rosina Ottolini's bakery, the only one admitted by the Military Police, did not remain inactive. It was located at the bottom of Via Cattaneo, at the fork with Via Olmata. Almost across from it, where there used to be Pasqualino Della Millia's grocer shop, there was even some competition from the American bakers, who were kneading buns and doughnuts. But, with the Germans at Campo di Carne, every bit of land was off limits for the civilians, who were by now suffering.

The Allied Military Government were not lacking in humanitarian scruples. They felt an obligation to protect the refugees, ship them off, feed them, disinfest them and send down to southern Italy, where there was enough room for them. A shipload had already sailed on 13th February, when evacuation was optional. Fate had willed it that Lucas and the population were to be united in their misfortune: the order to clear out was in fact given to both on the same day: Tuesday 22nd February.

Here we have another example of Don Steno's participation. It was he who warned the Nettuno and Anzio people, going around the countryside in a jeep, accompanied by one or two American officers. He called at the farmhouses and distributed or pasted on the walls the posters containing the order to leave. Each person could take with him only one bundle, nearly always bulging with clothes. There were some Venetians among them, who had experienced the migration of 1915-'18 and had dreamed of an 'Eldorado' in a land contending with malaria. With their mattresses on their backs, they showed up at the St. Teresa refugee centre, where they were divided into groups.

The wait before embarking, was rarely short. Many had to camp for days in the Anzio church which still stood, undamaged, aside the bomb craters. American lorries collected the civilians from the countryside, from Sacro Cuore Church and from St. Rocco's: gathering points of the Nettuno people, and picked them also from St. Teresa's to the port. The operation was completed on Ester Sunday and Monday, 9th and 10th April. Not less than ten thousand people left and we have been handed down a symbol of their separation: some elderly people bent down and picked up a handful of sand, wrapping it in a handkerchief as a relic of their world, perhaps never to be seen again.

However off the port of Naples, the city lights, no longer subjected to the black-out, were like a life-giving injection. On land, they all had to strip down in a barracks and present themselves naked to be sprayed with DDT, and under a shower complete the extermination of lice and fleas; they had never managed to laugh at the amusing aspects of that depressing procedure. Ester Monday was actually festive. The corvette Brooklyn As 220, had decked itself out with flags, in the middle of the Bay of Naples to signal the presence of one more passenger on board. Santa Cecconi Camilli, evacuees from Piscina Cardillo district, was responseble for all this festivity: she had just given birth to a boy. The baby was given the name of the sailor, Giorgio, who, together with Marcella Lopez (the godmother from Cisterna), held him during the Christening. The most important role had however been played by another sailor, the Italian-American Antonio

Sa-varese who, with his knowledge of pharmacy, had helped Santa to give birth.

From another ship, a few days before, the mortally sick Marisa Taurelli, Tony's younger sister, had been taken ashore. In the hut of Seccia area, the evening that the Americans had come to collect the evacuees, she had knocked over a patrol lamp and set herself on fire. She had been taken to the Hospital for Incurable with third-degree burns. Tony had rushed down from Bagnoli to see her. He returned to the hospital after given the farewell to the 504th only to find the bed empty and his mother crying.

Tony stayed in Naples until the liberation of Rome, joining a detachment of American Engineers who were busy fixing up the port. After the war, in 1987, Lt. Navas came to Nettuno and presented him with a gold medal, with these words: "Your spirit and your courage were an inspiration for every one of us. You were with me during my last reconnaissance, on 27th February 1944, when I lost my left arm. I'll never forget it".

ANZIO-NETTUNO BEACH HEAD

A meeting- conference at the Military Police headquarters in Via Romana, at Nettuno. From left: Mario Ottolini, local food expert, Capt. A. Mack, Prince Steno Borghese, Major Ridgway B. Knight, Senior Civil Affair Office, and Rodrigo Taurelli, with the Police armband.

ANZIO-NETTUNO BEACH HEAD

Prince Borghese (right), with his father WWI helmet, had been acting as mayor by the Commissioner of Nettunia (Anzio-Nettuno) after the order of evacuation during the German occupation and he was kept by the Allied Command to look after the population. In the picture some refugee on their way to be taken by trucks which will take them to the harbor of Anzio for embarking to south.

ANZIO-NETTUNO BEACH HEAD

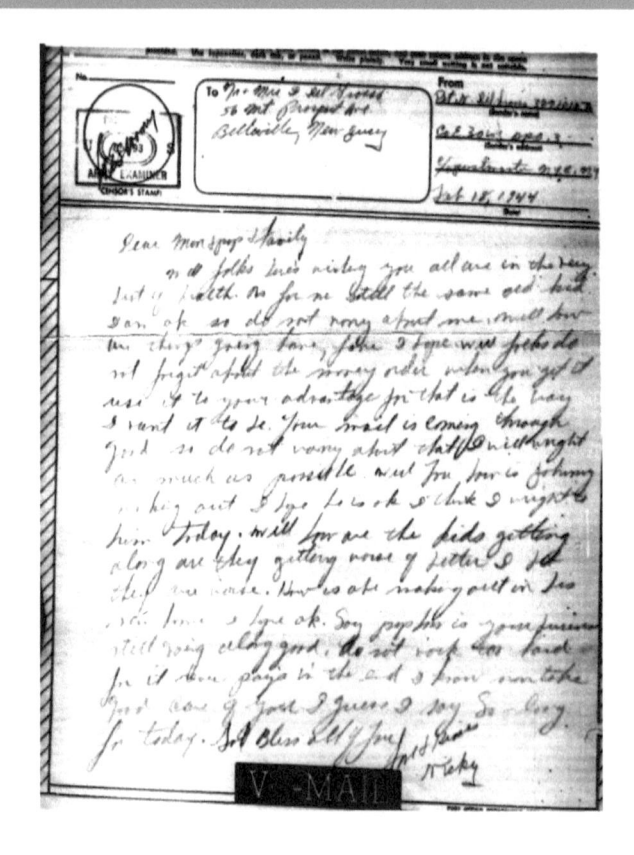

The last letter written by the Italo-American soldier Pvt. Nicholas J. Del Grosso, E Co. 2nd Battalion, 30th Infantry, 3rd Division, to his parents in Belleville, New Jersey, the 18th February, 1944. He was 19 years old and he was killed two days later, 20th February, along with other 128 infantrymen in the area between Padiglione tower and the Factory (Aprilia). His mother Adelaide, which emigrated to Usa in 1903, from Benevento, Italy, with her husband Ignazio, died 9 months later. Because the death of Nicholas caused her to suffer extreme Hypertension.

COLLECTING DOORS AND WINDOWS

Nothing must be forgotten. The historians' books glide over the period, nearly three months, from the beginning of March to 22nd May, when the two boxers at Nettuno-Anzio, after the swings and clinches, temporarily lowered their gloves. The public outside found this break monotonous. But that period, dismissed with only a few lines as one of calm, was a period of brutalization for those who were on the inside. The war correspondent Ernie Pyle, pseudonym for Ernest Taylor, who subsequently died in the Pacific during an assault by the Marine, wrote: "...The soldiers I met in the front line was a man who lived like an animal...He lived in filth, ate if and when he could, slept on the bare ground, without a roof over his head... Those who ignored these facts had no right to be impatient over the slowness of the march towards Rome".

The 500-600 civilians authorized to stay behind in the beach-head were not spared from this prolonged situation. Nearly all of them worked with the Americans who, by the way, soon after the landing, had already made a start on the construction of that monumental work which was to become their cemetery. It was on the land which had been expropriated from the Brovellis, Pirris,

Isgros, Palladinis and Pietrobonis, all of them were later compensated by the Italian Government. A group of Italian soldiers who were quartered at La Chiusa di San Giacomo, helped in the excavating, along with about 100 German prisoners. Of the Nettuno-Anzio people, even after they had been obliged to evacuate, there was one who stayed on: Antonio Combi, a gardener at the cemetery, up to the day of his retirement.

The Americans, however, suspected that agents were hiding on the farms, mingling among the few farmers who had been left behind to look after the livestock. The outcome was another turn of the screw by the Military Police which, urged to eliminate espionage, did not split hairs over making arrests. There was more than one blunder. They arrested Ernesto Astorino at Campo di Bove, put a 'prisoner of war' sign around his neck and then locked him in an enclosure with the Nazis and fascists behind the walls of St. Teresa's, simply because the spoke German and possessed a radio. Cpt. Charles Forte interrogated him. Ernesto, like a bright student with a good knowledge of English, had no trouble explaining himself: "I made the radio with a galena crystal, and besides, it only receives and does not transmit".

They escorted him back home, loading him with provisions. Mario Eufemi was quicly released, just like Ernesto. He had been arrested on 7th May with Angelo Catanzani. As civil servants of Nettuno-Anzio, they were accused of belonging to the Fascist party. When they were searched, something compromising emerged from Angelo's pockets: a letter addressed by him to his sister and brother-in-law, who were evacuated down south, to inform them on family affair: "The Americans have occupied the vineyard, placing cannons and weapons everywhere". Just what the MP was looking for. Angelo, who wasn't even given the chance to defense himself, was imprisoned for a whole month in Naples.

The houses of Anzio-Nettuno were also searched and completely stripped in those last months. The request for aid to the population which, on 18th November 1944, Don Steno had sent to Myron Taylor, Roosevelt's Ambassador to the holy See, was based on the following: "The necessity of each soldiers, who could not stay in town, to build a shelter in the open country, and such is the case for hundreds of thousands of soldiers who have joined forces and followed one another to the same highly restricted territory, has forced them to look for material to make their shelters safer. They have therefore taken from unoccupied dwelling all the doors, windows, shutters, wardrobe doors, gates, string bed, wood and whatever else could serve to cover their fox-holes".

Everything else, outside the town, had been thrown into utter confusion by more than just the explosions. The vineyards and wheat fields had been ploughed up, the brush had been given over to tanks, vehicles and ammunition and fuel deposits, among thousands of holes which, as Don Steno angrily pointed out, when he asked for medicines and machines for leveling the ground, risked becoming with the rains breeding-grounds for malaria and epidemics. Truscott had hoped to be able to get out of here quickly with a maneuver known as Operation Panther, planned for 19th March. The go-ahead should have come from Cassino. But the Germans re-emerged from the craters open by the ton-loads of bombs and succeeded in driving back not only the English, but also the New Zealand Army under General Freyberg and the Indians.

That was the end of Operation Panther, which was supposed to have broken the Gustav Line. Churchill, who had been counting on a reunion with the isolated Truscott, could not hide his disappointment from Alexander: "I wish you would explain to me why this passage by Cassino Monastery Hill, etc..., all on a front of two or three miles, is the only place which you must keep butting at". Alexander replied with a report which the Prime Minister deemed exhaustive, and concluded: "We must get ready to attack on a wider front and above all, wait for the snow to melt from the mountains".

Once again, a sort of smoke screen, made possible by the ability of Allied security and intelligence services, stopped Kesserling from foreseeing what was about to happen to him. Alexander was able to secretly gather his divisions, taking from the Adriatic the bulk of the Eighth Army, while the Germans, expecting another landing at Civitavecchia of Livorno or Tarquinia or even Ostia, were spreading their forces around. They also believed that it would have been impossible for the Anglo-American to launch another offensive between Cassino and the sea, before 24th May.

The offensive, which carried the code name Operation Diadem, was launched on 11th May, when even General Heinrich Vietinghoff-Scheel, commander of the 10th Army, on the Gustav Line, had absented himself to go and receive a decoration from Hitler at Berchtesgaden. Senger un Etterlin, the Bavarian general who had done the most to force the New Zealander Freyberg back, was also on leave, so was General E.G. Baade, defender of the bastion north-west of

Montecassino, and Siegfried Westphal, Kesserling's right arm. On the other hand, Alexander put in some overtime, having rushed back to Nettuno-Anzio to confirm all the moves with Truscott.

Truscott showed him the four plans he had prepared according to Clark's orders: Operation Grasshopper; Operation Crawdad; Operation Turtle and Operation Buffalo. The latter, which contemplated a thrust at Cisterna, and advance towards Valmontone (south of the Alban Hills), and the occupation of the Highway N. 6 (the Casilina) so as to cut off the retreat of the German 10th Army from Cassino, obtained the approval of Alexander, who was totally unaware of the rest of hornets he was about to plunge into. Once he came to know of it, Clark rushed to Via Romana to give Truscott a first warning: "The capture of Rome is the only important objective". With Alexander, he turned it into a procedure issue, telling him over the telephone that he did not want to be overridden: "I would be grateful if all orders to the Fifth Army could go through me".

So, it's the usual situation, that is, the onset of a third misunderstanding or 'squeeze' after those regarding the dispositions (modified) to Lucas and the use (disregarded) of the paratroopers. Unable to foresee all this, Alexander confirmed to

ANZIO-NETTUNO BEACH HEAD

Churchill at 11 o' clock on 11th May what they both yearned for: "The operation to chase the Germans away from Cassino and destroy their army south of Rome had got under way".

The Polish Army had some trouble at the offset, while General Juin's Maroccan soldiers scaled the mountains and took Mount Maio in less than 48 hours. On 17th May, the red and white Polish flag was flying over the abbey ruins, and while units of the Eighth Army were preparing to break the fortified line between Pontecorvo and Aquino (named 'Adolf Hitler' by the Todt Organization), and the Americans were pressing the Germans on the Formia coast, Churchill cabled Alexander: "I congratulate you on the fine advance made along your whole front. Please inform me now when you intend attacking at Anzio-Nettuno".

Alexander, as usual, explained everything properly: "We have led the Germans to believe that our offensive would be leaving from the beach-head, now that they have taken out two divisions (the 90th and the 26th), gone to the Liri Valley, we can give Truscott the go-ahead. We feel that, to be on the safe side, his attack should coincide with the breaking of the Adolf Hitler Line". On 23rd May, the Canadians from the Eighth Army risked an attack on that line. The same morning, at 5:45, the starting whistle for the match was given by cannons firing from outside Nettuno, in the direction of Cisterna. An English skirmish across the mouth of the Moletta, est of Anzio, had already been staged to distract the enemy.

On the eve of the breakout, Clark from his Fifth Army Advance headquarters in Villa Borghese, held a conference to make it clear, according to the fairly malicious conclusion of the journalists, that from that moment on, operations should be personally guided by him. Unlike Prince Condê, he didn't get much sleep that night. He was already on his feet at 4:30 a.m. then he waited at an artillery base with Truscott for the curtain to go up, without revealing that he was contemplating the possibility of reversing course.

The attack, in the direction of Velletri, was made by Harmon's Armored Division and O'Daniel 3rd Infantry Division towards Cisterna. It was protected on the left by the 45th Eagles Division, and on the right, by a brigade which, behind the rather bureaucratic label of First Special Service Force concealed some of the most irregular and at the same time heroic products of the US Army in the Second World War. It was commanded by General Robert Frederick, a 35 years old, native of San Francisco. He had personally created the brigade and trained if in Montana, recruiting Americans and Canadians, even prisoners: "I need men who are rough, brutal, ready for anything, aware of having few chances of taking their hide back home".

This gang, trained to parachute and ski, was supposed to have sabotaged the hydroelectric plant in Norway that supplied Germany. When this plan was cancelled, they were landed on the Aleutian Island to fight against the Japanese. Then they were dispatched to Italy Their bunks on the ship that brought them to Anzio-Nettuno on 1st February were brightened by the presence of a unit of prostitutes invited on board by Sgt. Jake Walkmeister. However, on the battlefield these chaps proved to be invincible. Frederick's speed in maneuvering; and his contempt of danger caused Churchill to utter: "With a dozen men like him, we could have defeated Hitler back in 1942".

In short, on 23rd May, this bold man and his unit of former jailbirds (not all of them, of course) broke through the German line, beyond the Moscarello (Mussolini) Canal and advanced as far as the Appia, Highway N. 7, elbowing their way like an attacking forefront among opposing full-backs. The 3rd Division was surrounding Cisterna. Harmon, beyond the Femminamorta Creek, was pushing his Sherman tanks towards the Velletri-Valmontone crossing. Kesserling was beginning to quarrel with von Mackensen who, more malleable than himself, was ready to give in immediately.

ANZIO-NETTUNO BEACH HEAD

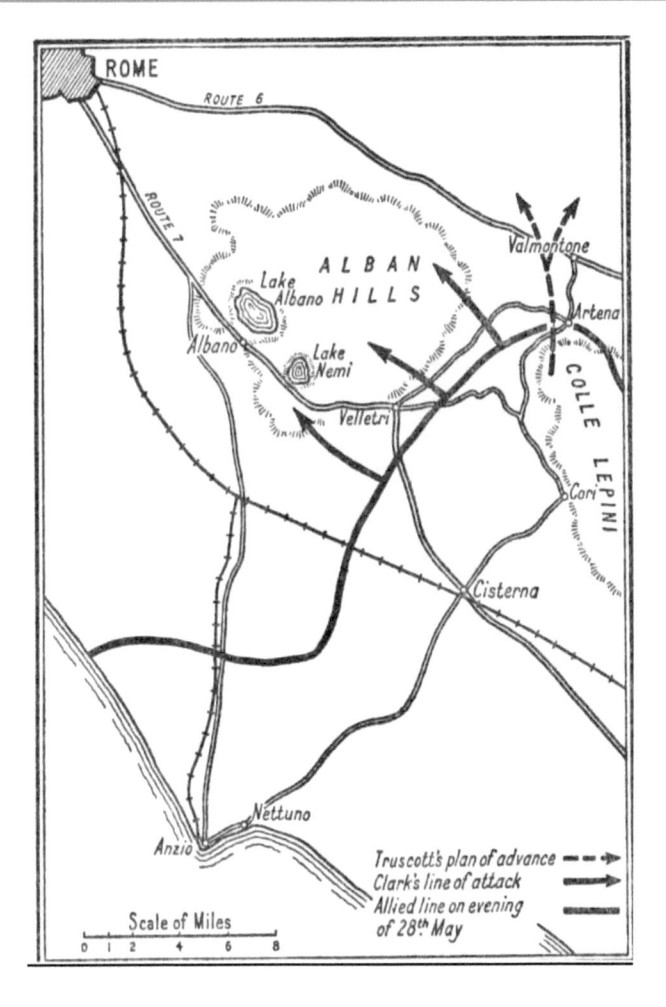

The 6th Corps, encouraged by the fall of Cassino made the attack in May 23 -25 and broke the siege at Cisterna and, at last, they could join up with General Clark's Fifth Army on their way to capture Rome.

ANZIO-NETTUNO BEACH HEAD

The last attack by the Germans, then concentrated at Cisterna, was launched against Nettuno-Anzio at the end of February. The American defense (represented in the photograph by the three infantrymen of the 3rd Division), was not unaware and they drove the Germans back. From then on, until 23rd May, it was a war of position.

ANZIO-NETTUNO BEACH HEAD

Cisterna completed demolished, as it appear to the forefront of the 3rd Division who got the German surrender.

ANZIO-NETTUNO BEACH HEAD

On the announcement that Rome was liberated there was a rush to return home started by whatever means available. From Naples, Salerno, Irpinia, Calabria, Sicily, with the Allied ships no longer at their disposal, several Anzio-Nettuno people set off on foot, trusting in a chance lift which didn't always materialize. Maria Onori Colaceci, barefoot, seems to want to wipe out the ugliness of the war.

ANZIO-NETTUNO BEACH HEAD

Cpl. Joe Quinn, with trumpet, plays the farewell to the cities of Anzio and Nettuno, not only to his comrade in arms Sgt. Robert Lewis, Sgt. John Ferris and Cpl. Thomas Flynn, on a sea summer boat, but also to all the soldiers leaving the area. Not all could make a return trip back home, many of them rest here in the military cemeteries.

ANZIO-NETTUNO BEACH HEAD

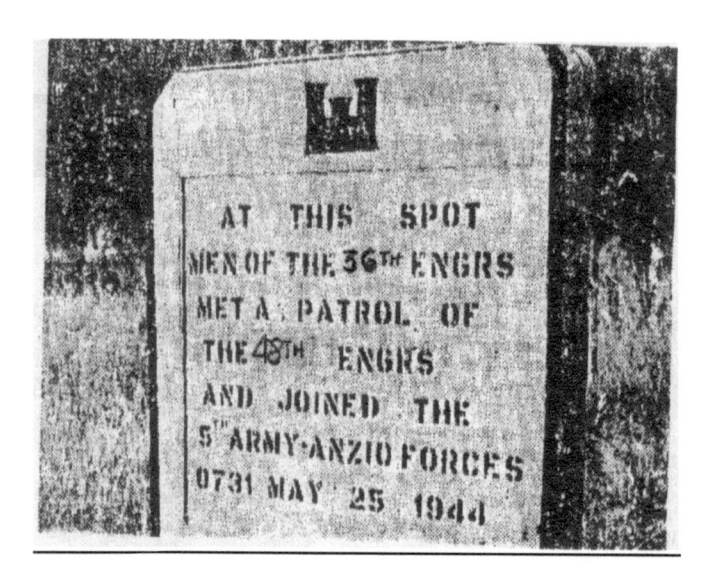

> AT THIS SPOT
> MEN OF THE 36TH ENGRS
> MET A PATROL OF
> THE 48TH ENGRS
> AND JOINED THE
> 5TH ARMY-ANZIO FORCES
> 0731 MAY 25 1944

Borgo Grappa (18 miles east from Anzio-Nettuno): On the exact spot where the 5th Army main forces and beachhead troops were joined, this marker was erected in May 1944. In the history of the entire war, this spot was forgotten, but for the men of the 5th it was important because it meant the end of the beachhead as such and turned the army into a united force which could push on Rome with greater strength than before. It was the end of the beachhead. "Hell on Hearth". Names of the units which participated in the meeting had been eliminated by the censor. ("Star and Stripes" - June 3, 1944; "The Watch on the Rhine" - 3rd Infantry Division Association Magazine, December 1994 issue, p.17 by Jack Ellis, Historian).
May 25th, 1944 – 07:31 a.m.

THE DRAMATIC MEETING

Cisterna did not fall straight away. It was still resisting on the 24th, but O'Daniel's infantry was able to go beyond it and take the Cori slopes. Truscott no longer had any doubt: he was overcoming the team that had held him in check for months. That evening, he received a second warning from Clark: "Have you thought about the possibility of a deviation from Valmontone?". "Of course, if the enemy realizes the danger it is facing here, and reroutes the forces, we steer for the Alban Hills". "Very well, let's consider this possibility".

On the following day, Truscott quickly became convinced that, on the contrary, it should be rejected, what was left of Cisterna, that so heavily blasted and flattened Cisterna, finally evacuated, was a line of smoke, prolonged and slow like the breathing of someone being resuscitated. Meanwhile, Frederick's brigade after climbing Mount Artemisio had got past Cori and were racing so fast towards Rocca Massima and Artena that they lost contact with the 3rd Division and exposed themselves to the German attacks on their flanks. Also nearly in the morning there was the historic meeting at Borgo Grappa, when a patrol of

American engineers and English surveyors on reconnaissance between Borgo Sabotino and Fogliano Lake, met a patrol of US 2nd Corps, which had already captured Fondi and Terracina, and was then leaving Circeo mountain behind. Cpt. Ben Souza from Honolulu and Lt. Francis Buckley from Philadelphia, had to repeat the scene of the dramatic meeting for the photographers when Clark arrived with the journalists.

But, with the success of the tanks, Truscott had to proof that Operation Buffalo was about to ensnare the Germans. Some of Harmon's tanks had difficulty in getting right to Velletri nut another column, commanded by Colonel Hamilton Houze, had found an opening in the valley east of the city, which led to Valmontone. It was Clark's fault that that opening was not exploited. In the late afternoon, General Donald W. Brann, one of the Fifth Army commander's aides, was waiting for Truscott outside the command post: "The Boss want you to mount the assault north-west and send only the 3rd Division with Frederick's men to Valmontone. He mentioned it to you yesterday...". Truscott was dumbfounded. He asked him to repeat the order. "I can't believe it", he protested, "I want to speak to him before abandoning the entire plan. This was not my original agreement with Clark. We had discussed an hypothesis that did not materialize. Nevertheless, we can wipe out the retreating German Army on the Casilina Highway N.6".

Clark was nowhere to be found. No one knew where he had got to. Truscott could not talk to him and had no choice but to obey. At Valmontone the Germans still had a way of escape. The way to Rome, shorter according to the maps, if one followed the Appia Highway N. 7, proved in practice to be longer for the Americans. On the morning of 26th May, the day on which the BBC correspondent Vaughan-Thomas broadcast his last news from Anzio-Nettuno: "The beach-head has ceased to exist", Truscott headed once more for Campoleone and Lanuvio with Harmon's tanks and the 45th, 34th and 36th Divisions. The latter, a reformed Texas division under the command of General Fred Walker, was the last to arrive in Nettuno-Anzio, but redeemed itself four days after the Rapido River debacle by discovering an opening through which to get up Mount Artemisio and take the Germans who were blocked in Velletri from the behind.

Alexander was faced with a *'fait accompli'*. Clark did not show his face to him, either. He sent Alexander the news with General Alfred Gruenter, his Chief of General Staff: "We believe that the Germans could no longer hold out on the Anzio side, therefore Clark thought it was better to charge them here". Alexander reacted with a smile. A few years later, he was baring his teeth in quite a different fashion. "If Clark had carried out my plan, Valmontone would have been the Germans disaster. I expected the load of publicity promised by the capture of Rome led him to switch the direction of his advance".

Alexander was himself tempted by the publicity. When he met Clark on 2nd June, they exchanged some strong words, precisely over the Eternal City. The American general, in a interview to Sydney T. Matthews in 1948, enlarged on the episode with disconcerting details. He confessed to having behaved like a cowboy with Alexander, who had wanted to include the Eighth Army in the march on Rome: "I told him that I would refuse to obey to such and order and if the Eighth Army tried to advance I would have my troops fire on them".

After the turnabout at Valmontone, ten days went by before the Americans entered Rome. Held in the Washington Archives there is an affidavit by General Frederick: "At dawn on June 4th, 1944, at 6:20 the forefront of the attacking troops, made up of elements from the 1st Special Service Force and elements of the 1st Armored Division entered the outskirt of Rome". For Churchill, the first goal was another: "At 7:15 p.m. on June 4th the head of the

US 88th Division entered the Piazza Venezia, in the heart of the capital.

Alexander would have preferred not only to avoid a special bulletin on Rome, but to have just thrown it in with all the other 'inhabited localities' taken by day. Churchill made him understand he would be covering himself with ridicule: "The conquest of Rome is an event of world-wide importance and should not be minimized". The Prime Minister's qualities were evident, especially when it was a question of putting on a good front. While Clark was parked with his jeep in St. Peter's Square, Churchill cabled Alexander: "I congratulate you and ask you to compliment on our behalf the leaders and the troops of the United States, Great Britain, Canada, New Zealand, South Africa, India, France, Poland and Italy, who have distinguished themselves from one end of the line to the others". For us, who had failed everything up till then, this was the first report with a pass in democracy. The sacrifices at Anzio, Nettuno, Cisterna, Campo di Carne, Aprilia, Campoleone, Lanuvio and Latina had not been in vain. But was the landing truly necessary? We would not be discussing the issue, had the Valmontone trap (another goal opportunity missed) functioned. Hitler has been given all the credit for saving Rome because, on 2nd June when Kesserling requested that the city be evacuated without resistance, he replied: "Very well: it is a centre of culture to be respected". But perhaps this would not have been immediately granted without pressure from the 6th Corps.

Furthermore, the balance with which Churchill consoled himself is not insignificant. On 5th June, under the heading 'From the Prime Minister to Prime Minister Stalin' London transmitted to Moscow a very lengthy message that can be summarized as follow: "Although the amphibious landing at Anzio and Nettuno did not immediately fructify as I had hoped when it was planned, it was a correct strategic move, and brought its reward in the end. First, it drew ten German divisions from the following places: one from France, one from Hungary, four from Yugoslavia, one from Denmark, and three from North Italy". (Churchill, *Op. cit.*, p. 539).

The Normandy landing took place only 24 hours later, Not for nothing did the name Nettuno (Neptune) figure among the many code names used to safeguard the secrecy of this colossal operation. The name which had been suppressed by decree N. 1958 dated 27 November 1939, signed by Victor Emmanuel III and sanctioning the fusion of Nettuno and Anzio into Nettunia, was about to come back to life with the signature of Victor Emmanuel's son Umberto, who had been appointed lieutenant of the kingdom, precisely on 5th June. Nearly a year later, on 3rd May 1945, less than a month before the referendum proclaiming the republic, the head of the government Bonomi and the Minister of Justice Tupini signed together with Umberto, decree N. 265 by which Anzio became Anzio once more, and Nettuno returned to being Nettuno.

More than re-affirming their identity, the Nettuno and Anzio people needed to recover the ownership of their lost 'eden'. On the announcement that Rome had been liberated, there was a rush to return home, started from whatever means available. From Naples, Salerno, Irpinia, Calabria, Sicily, with the Allied ships no longer at their disposal, several Nettuno-Anzio people set off on foot, trusting in a chance lift which didn't always materialize. Eugenio Ottaviani, having thus dragged himself on foot from Cicciano, near Nola, had to spend four days in bed on account of the blisters on his feet. Likewise Lello Bellobono and his two sons: Franco and Mario; and his brother Angelo Bellobono with his son Guglielmo, all of them evacuees in Castellamare di Stabia. It took them five days to get back to Nettuno, by marching on the Appia Highway, through Fondi, Terracina, Borgo S.Michele. Guglielmo lost at Fondi the military boots which he had taken off to rest his feet and they were stolen by someone passing by.

The Madonna of Grace, also returned. The 'Lady of Ipswich' as she was known in England, was taken to Rome for safety, as we have seen, and there the Nettuno and Anzio people could go and pray; another devoted from faraway, actually from Ipswich itself, was on the search of her, maybe because of a promise made at home. Remo Frasca, a 14 years old from Nettuno recalls: "I was just wondering around in the S. Rocco Square, to see if some of my friends was waiting to be taken to the port of Anzio for the journey to south. That day nobody was there and while making a turn on myself to go back to the vineyard where my family still stood, I was approached by an English soldier. Although he spoke not a word of Italian and my English vocabulary consisted of few words, we somehow managed to communicate. He showed me a medal with the image of the Madonna of Grace: "Where is she?", he asked me. "The statue is no longer in the church, she is in Rome", I told the young soldiers, then we said goodbye to each other".

Now on September 9th, 1944 decorated with flowers, carried on a small lorry and accompanied by Don Nicola, Don Vincenzo, and the Passionists Friars Mauro, Tito, Pietro, and Gerardo, the holy statue was coming back. The joint population of Nettuno-Anzio was waiting outside St. Teresa's Church. The Madonna arrived at 3 p.m. The Anzio people carried her on their shoulders up to the borderline with Nettuno, at the end of Viale Mencacci, and it was then the turn of the Nettuno people again in procession, to return her to the home in St. Rocco's Church.

The Madonna's presence was more than ever needed. After five months of German occupation and four of war at home. The population was starting again from scratch.

ANZIO-NETTUNO BEACH HEAD

U.S. Third Infantry Division Monument, built in June 1944, in Foglino Wood – Nettuno, with the inscription: "U.S. Third Infantry Division made an assault amphibious landing in this vicinity, established a beachhead which was maintained for four months at great sacrifice of human life and with indomitable courage in a valiant and sanguinary attack the division led an offensive that destroyed the strong German defenses and culminated in the liberation of Rome".

ANZIO-NETTUNO BEACH HEAD

Silvano Casaldi's family has ancient origins in Nettuno, Italy. He was born in Teggiano, in the province of Salerno, in 1944, during the invasion of the Anzio-Nettuno Beachhead. After the Anglo-American landing of 22 January 1944 his family had been evacuated and returned to Nettuno, Italy, in July of '44, a month after the liberation of Rome. At that time Silvano was only two months and fifteen days in age.

He grew up in the medieval town where his father opened a workshop in Piazza G. Marconi N. 8. His family, who lived in via XXV Luglio, found the house damaged by bombing and rented an apartment in via Forno a Soccio, N. 4, in the Borgo. Later he moved to Via A. Ongaro, N. 3, here in the medieval town, in the area of the San Giovanni's church, the father, grandfather and earlier ancestors of Silvano were born.

Following his passion for the study of foreign languages, he enrolled at the hotel college in Castel Fusano in 1962. After a year of study and theory he was employed at the Cavalieri Hilton hotel in Rome, inaugurated in 1963, between Via Trionfale and Viale Medaglie d' Oro. He worked in Switzerland in the German canton (Beckenried - Lucerne); England (Manchester) and Canada (Montreal).

Returning to Nettuno in 1969 he found employment at the Colgate Palmolive industrial plant, until 1974, when he was hired by the Municipality of Nettuno as a Vigile Urbano (Town Police) interpreter and then in 1984 was employed at the Tourist Office.

History and culture have been his passion since then. His first book, "Those Days in Nettuno" was written in both languages Italian and English in 1989, together with the journalist Francesco Rossi, in order to show that the name of Nettuno must be added to the war event commonly known as the landing of Anzio. It was, however, a sort of historical investigation that deserved the introduction and approval of Prof. Giovanni Spadolini (Chairman of the Senate Republic of Italy).

In 1990 he opened "The Allied Landing Museum", for the Municipality of Nettuno, the first Italian Museum dedicated to the landing of 22 January 1944. For his work he met three presidents of the United States of America. George Bush senior, Bill Clinton and Gerald Ford. To Gerald Ford he acted as a guide during the visit to the American Cemetery of Nettuno. Oscar Luigi Scalfaro, during his term as president of the Italian Republic appointed him Commendatore al Merito della Repubblica (Knight Commander), in 1995.

He won the "Lucus Feroniae" Award in 1997.
In 2013 he won "Il Tridente d'Oro - Città di Anzio e Nettuno" award.

ANZIO-NETTUNO BEACH HEAD

British Sherwood Foresters Regiment Monument, built in July 1944, now in Villa Adele's Park – Anzio, with the inscription: Campoleone – Puntoni – Buon Riposo – Fosso Acqua Buona – "At the going down of the sun and in the morning we will remember them".

Also by Silvano Casaldi

Quei giorni a Nettuno/Those Days at Nettuno
(Italian/English Edition)

La storia del Nettuno Calcio

Come eravamo

Gli uomini dello sbarco/The Men of the Landing
Anzio/Nettuno 22 gennaio 1944
(Italian/English Edition)

Me no vo' ì all'America

Nettuno – Una storia fotografica

Nettuno e le sue priore

Un avvocato d'altri tempi

Nettuno nell'inferno dello sbarco

Altri ricordi di Nettuno

Quei giorni a Nettuno

ANZIO-NETTUNO BEACH HEAD

Sembra strano però
Romanzo

Incontri a Rionegro
Romanzo

Change of Heart (Sembra strano però)
English Edition
Romance

ANZIO-NETTUNO BEACH HEAD

Made in United States
Troutdale, OR
09/07/2023